LV

D0794388

$5 \times \frac{9}{10} (2/06)$
$7 \times \frac{10}{10} (4/10)$

Lichtenberg
and
the Little
Flower Girl

Also by Gert Hofmann

BALZAC'S HORSE AND OTHER STORIES

BEFORE THE RAINY SEASON

THE FILM EXPLAINER

*LUCK

OUR CONQUEST

THE PARABLE OF THE BLIND

THE SPECTACLE AT THE TOWER

*Available from New Directions

Lichtenberg and the Little Flower Girl

GERT HOFMANN

Translated and with an Afterword by
MICHAEL HOFMANN

 A NEW DIRECTIONS BOOK

Published by arrangement with Carl Hanser Verlag and with the kind assistance of Jennifer Lyons of Writers House, and with Michael Hofmann.

Manufactured in the United States of America
New Directions Books are printed on acid-free paper.
First published clothbound in 2004
Published simultaneously in Canada by Penguin Books Canada Limited

Library of Congress Cataloging-in-Publication Data

Hofmann, Gert.
[Kleine Stechardin. English]
Lichtenberg and the Little Flower Girl / Gert Hofmann ; translated from the German and with an afterword by Michael Hofmann.
    p. cm.
ISBN 0-8112-1568-7 (alk. paper)
I. Hofmann, Michael, 1957 Aug. 25–   II. Title.
PT2668.0376K5713   2004
833'.914—dc22   2003028140

New Directions Books are published for James Laughlin
by New Directions Publishing Corporation
80 Eighth Avenue, New York, NY 10011

Contents

Lichtenberg
and
the Little
Flower Girl

IT WILL NOT HAVE ESCAPED ADMIRERS OF LICHTENBERG that many of the things attributed to him in this book have been quite shamelessly invented and concocted: his sitting around in the evenings, the back and forth—mainly forth—of his feelings, the regular headaches, and the irregular quotations. But it is precisely here, in the inventions and concoctions, the conundrums and contradictions, the whole—as someone once put it—"human mess," that the full truth about the little man may find its best expression. Under our hands, he has become not as he was, but as he might also have been.

GERT HOFMANN

1.

*O*NCE, MANY MANY YEARS AGO, Professor Lichten-berg pulled on his lecture coat and headed out. He wanted to see what the weather was doing. Because he was a vain fellow, he had silver buttons on his lecture coat. From time to time, he would lose one. Then he would go crawling around his apartment in the wing of the house on the Gotmarstrasse, crying: Where has it got to now? As he scrabbled around among the chair legs, one thing became clear: he had a hunchback! Quick, let's write about it!

The hunchback was enormous!

Lichtenberg himself can't have been much taller than four-foot-nine. And that's how he would go about in the world. That's how he would go about in the public street, and even out of town. But he always came back. Sometimes he would wear a hat, mostly he wouldn't. They called him "a little lizard of a fellow" or "our leprechaun."

He would never have been good-looking, even without a hunchback. His eyes were generally inflamed, his nose dripped from time to time, people corresponded about his ears—"like dishcloths!"—and as for his teeth . . . More about them anon! His hunchback was a little beast that squatted on top of him. From there it dominated his life. Even the agitation that came over him from time to time came from there. People didn't just want to see it, they were keen to touch it as well.

What for?

Because it was lucky!

And so he trotted through the town. Stop, little chappie, they cried, and reached out their hands towards his hunchback. He wished they wouldn't insist on touching it. It made him feel terribly impatient, later sad.

Stop that, he cried, what do you think you're doing? Sometimes he ran away.

He had vile thoughts when he was sitting alone at home, writing one of his long and witty letters to a young and pretty woman. He sucked the top of his pen and thought them . . . He would be wearing a wig, usually one of human hair. He wore silver buckles on his shoes. When he had been walking awhile, he cried: Air! and pulled them open. Because the wig was a little big for him—"look," he said, "my head's shrinking!"—he tugged at it from time to time. Under his arm he carried a bunch of books "that double, if not treble, the significance of the world." And now I'm going to bring the world back to manageable proportions, he cried, and tore out a few pages. Often he hated scholarliness and got all melancholy. He sat in a corner and cried: What's it all for? (He meant life and all the trimmings.) And now, he said, I'll take a turn round the block! The students he called his "little ones." I can already hear them stamping their feet with impatience, he said! Any minute I'll have to start earning money and spreading understanding!

That was . . .

In May 1777. It's no longer true. It has to be made up afresh.

And where?

Why, in Göttingen on the Leine! Where the professor lived. And his books and scientific equipment with him.

His eyesight got worse. Sometimes he couldn't see anything, sometimes admittedly too much. Then he would shut his eyes and cry: That much isn't called for! His round head rather thoughtful, he hadn't been out yet that day. He preferred indoors. There he had his three desks and any number of chairs and the colossal bookcase "that one day will fall on top of me." And the windows, affording him a view of the street, and of those people who were coming down it, perhaps with a view to seeing him. (It was the custom for artists and scholars to keep open house, and offer all comers a plate of soup.) "It is characteristic of Göttingen," he wrote to Johann Gottwerth Müller von Itzehoe (1743–1828) "that even the outdoors are cramped, to say nothing of the Göttingen minds!" Because he wasn't in England anymore—and wouldn't go there again—he stopped looking out of the window. All he could see there was the German sky anyway, more white than blue.

So Lichtenberg sat in Göttingen with few friends and numerous adversaries.

And without so much as a wife?

Without a wife!

When he set foot outside the house, there was a small puff of wind blowing. The Gotmarstrasse was almost empty. The wind swept the hat off one gentleman's head, or at least it did its damnedest to. It lifted up the women's skirts, that was the best thing about the wind. Lichtenberg went out onto the street to keek under a skirt or two. To see the odd ankle and calf, and maybe even a knee. He thought: Nothing is wasted on me, not even trifles!

Was he really as tiny as people said, and as they wrote in London? Well, one thing, he had stopped growing! Or maybe his brain was still growing, he wasn't sure. His brow, when he passed his hand over it, was prettily curved, but what was behind it? At any rate, he had dainty little hands and feet, and shining eyes, sometimes. And that big head full of notions—"both scientific and other." With that, he invented an alternative world, which he often made notes about. Shame, he thought, that I'm not completely healthy!

What was the matter with the man?

Most often "an ague with fever." Then he pulled on his night-cap, and lay down in his wide empty bachelor's bed. There was a space next to him, but it wasn't possible to find a woman to occupy it. He pulled the blankets up to his throat, then his hunchback was gone. If his students came and called for him next door, he let them know: I'm grateful for the inexplicable popularity, but they're to leave me alone! I'm preoccupied with my body today, the other thing's closed! Or he was suffering from "hunchbackitis," which "left him incapable of the upright walk that is the leading characteristic of our species." Often when he should have been giving a lecture, his students had to go home empty-headed.

Once there was waiting for him in a coal-black coat a Professor Crome from Giessen, who revered him. "As his listeners," wrote Crome, "depressed by so much youthful learning, finally emerged from the lecture room, Lichtenberg tottered down from his chair, and fell unconscious into the arms of his manservant Pesti. Pesti carried the little man onto the chaise and laid him down. Thinking he was in convulsions and on the point of death, I didn't want to disturb him further and was about to take my leave," wrote Crome. "But his man assured me that he suffered this condition after most of his lectures, and it would pass soon enough. So I stayed, and we had a long and cordial discussion about electricity in rabbits, dogs and other hirsute mammals."

At any rate, Lichtenberg lay in bed a lot, wrestling with death.

"In case Heaven should really consider it necessary to withdraw me from circulation and put out a new version," he wrote to his friend Polycarp Erxleben (1744–1777), "I would like to give it one or two useful bits of advice, in particular concerning the form of my body and the overall design of the whole thing. Straighter," he wrote, "altogether straighter!"

It was a peculiarity of his that he was forever having to set out his ideas. It was an urge contained in his large, round and now almost bald, head. That's why he was so driven, why he was always looking for this thing or that. Not buried treasures or wigs—he was always looking for them too—but words, words! When he had found one, he would write it down on a piece of paper. He would take it over to the window. Then he would shake his head and say: No, not that one! and crossed it all out again. He was always on the lookout for something, for instance, cheap writing paper. Or a quill so he could scratch behind his ear. Or, continually, for a good friend, with whom he could walk, arm in arm, albeit rather lower, through the Barfusserstrasse, telling him the while what was on his mind. Or a mistress.

Eh? The little cripple?

Why ever not?

It was the eighteenth century, and he never managed to out-live it. He was now thirty-five years old and he looked in the mirror a lot. While there, he thought: I look younger! be-cause, as already noted, he was vain as well. In the evening, he wore his lined cap which kept his brain nice and warm. That's where all his desires were, his dreams, his thoughts. He didn't really believe in the other Being any more. But if he should have the grace, and if he really did acquire a mistress . . . Maybe he would sleep better? Maybe his hunchback would go away, just not be there after a while? "I should not shed," wrote Lichtenberg, "a single tear for it!"

Such was the yearning he carried about with him, first up the Gotmarstrasse, and then back down it again, on the opposite side. God, he thought, the weight of that yearning! and he pulled his wig down a little. Then his brow was covered, his temples were gone from sight. His heart was still pounding, though, because he was walking so fast.

Where to, in God's name?

To see his little ones. That would have been in 1777, more or less. Frederick the Great—the Great, is that right?—had invaded Bohemia with his forces. Unfortunately there were no battles. The Russians had got the better of the Turks on the Pruth, and now they occupied Wallachia. Lichtenberg sat around at home. He read books and wrote a little bit.

And he taught at the Kur Hanoverian University of Göttingen. That hadn't been in existence for very long. His lecture room was on the first floor, where he also lived, ate, slept, evacuated, and "had scientific dreams." Often he would have dreams of women as well. Then he would close his eyes and say: Oh! and they would file past him. When he saw one he liked the look of, he would dream of her for weeks. Then she would grow pale and dim, and another one came along. When he felt hungry during one of his lectures, he would say: I've had a scientific idea! And he would go to his kitchen and make himself some "very substantial" bread and butter. When he'd polished it off, he would return to his students, say: I'm back! and pick up just exactly where he'd left off. He had a hundred students. When he counted them sometimes, there were even a hundred and one. Or he only had ninety-nine, and he shook his head, because then someone would have overslept. Or one of them would have closed his eyes for the last time in the night. When it was time for the fellow to be buried, Lichtenberg exclaimed: Not that as well! He slipped into his black coat, got his boots polished, and trotted off to the cemetery. At the cemetery—it was the Nikolaikirche or else the Marienkirche—he would trot just behind the dead man, so as not to lose him in the crush. He remembered him, as he had known him and would now no longer see him. He tried to remember his nose, his fingers and the words he always used to say. Sometimes he would stand still for a moment and say: Yes, that's what he used to say! Then the coffin was lowered into the grave. Lichtenberg bowed the deepest and looked the longest. Pity, he thought, shook his head, and went home.

Among the students who hadn't died yet, he had a few sons of counts and earls, whom he needed to place advantageously in his lectures. These were von Meerbaum, von Amelung, Count Nauheim, Francis Clerke, baronet, and many others. Lichtenberg had powdered his chin. He had his gold watch in his fob-pocket and he flashed it. Anyone who had seen it flash, would also hear it tick. Sometimes it stopped. Well really, he said, and held it up to his ear. He was waiting for his noblemen's sons.

This way, Your Graces, called Lichtenberg, if you would kindly follow me! If Your Highnesses will permit, he said, and tugged them by the sleeve. His hands were bony and ever bonier. Invariably they were ice cold as well.

The Counts, in the flower of their youth, were well dressed and washed. They looked down upon him. He had to take them by the sleeve and pull them into the lecture room. Others preferred to be pushed. Once in the lecture room, they were seated one behind the other, in order of rank. Lichtenberg inquired: Are Your Highnesses sitting comfortably, or are there any complaints? They remained silent. Are Your Highnesses sitting comfortably, he repeated, and they thought about it for a while, and they said: Yes, we think we are sitting comfortably!

Well then, said Lichtenberg, and he wiped his brow. That was always damp. And can Your Highnesses hear everything I say?

We think we can hear everything!

And do you understand, asked Lichtenberg, do Your Highnesses understand the meaning of what I am saying, at least in general terms?

Oh yes, they cried, some of the time we do!

Then Lichtenberg took the latecomer Thomas Swanton, the admiral's son, by the hand, and led him to the front row of the lecture room, where he could keep an eye on him. When they got on to integration and Lichtenberg was explaining something tricky, he always fell asleep. When he walked, Lichtenberg always started wheezing, and his companion—Gleim, say, or Reimarus—would ask: Is it far to go?

No further than from the Maschmühle to the Weend Gate, Lichtenberg replied.

Is that far, they asked, and Lichtenberg: I think I can make it!

Such was his life at that time. Later on it would be a different one. If visitors came, he leapt up and called out: I'm not at home! Or: Hold on, I'm just coming! Then he opened the door. His visitor would doff his hat and say: Bonjour, mon ami! It might be Count Volta or Dr. Lessing or Dr. Blumenbach, who was a collector of skulls. Sometimes he would bring one. Lichtenberg asked: Have you got a new one? and Blumenbach said: Yes! Then he sat down, took it out of its bag, and passed it around. Sometimes it was an old man's, sometimes quite a young one's. Then it would still have its teeth, and Blumenbach demonstrated how firmly they were still attached. After that, he'd wrap it up in its brown paper again and set it aside. If it was raining, Lichtenberg took his little handkerchief—big ones hadn't been invented yet—and wiped the drops off his forehead. Yes, such was his life! He taught on the first floor of the Gotmarstrasse, which was sixteen steps up. He didn't complain, though. When he couldn't manage any more, he stopped and said: Oh, still more! and he pulled himself together. Every day—except Sunday, when it was trot along to the Jakobikirche and forty winks—he had to see to his students. He put his hand on the balustrade, and supported himself on it. After three or four steps, he said: Well, this isn't a bad start! If someone was coming up behind him, he let them overtake him, and said: Lead on, young friend, I'll follow! Later, when he got even sicker, he moved out to his little holiday cottage on the edge of town. It had a view of the graveyard, so he could watch his friends being buried. "Until the very end," he wrote, "they do everything in their power to impress me!"

At home he would stand by his garden gate until the Gotmarstrasse was unoccupied. He didn't want to show his hunchback. When there was nobody near, he said: I'll chance it! Then he ran out. In Spring, before St. John's Day, the birds sang in his garden, in winter it was quiet. He was wrapped in a cloak. He took out his wastebook and wrote: "Apparently they're coming back, the birds! It said so in the paper!" And he trotted on a bit further. Then he pulled out his wastebook again and wrote: "Not the same ones, of course, Nature's swapped them round."

Sometimes he went out in the garden. He thought of one or two women he wouldn't mind "leaping aboard, scaling, clambering about on top of," if only they would let him. But they didn't let him. He trampled on a couple of flowers, he had failed to notice them. When he saw what he had done, he said: Pardon me! If he intended to go out of town, he shouted for Bain-Marie and asked her to order him a carriage. To keep the cost down, he added: Just a small one! Then he drew the curtain, so he wasn't so easily spotted. Often he would be melancholy and say: No, I shan't get in! He would stand by the window and wait for it to get dark. He had his wig on, his coat buttoned up, his ideas all in place in his head, and it refused to get dark! How impatient I get when I'm waiting for it to get dark, he thought to himself, and looked up at the sky. Then he exclaimed: Enough already! and he stayed at home instead. How quickly progress was being made all over the world! In England they were assessing the effect of electricity on the growth of plants and animals. How it made everything shoot up! Only cats failed to thrive and shrivelled up!

When Lichtenberg, in his slippers, trotted along to his lecture, he wheezed and gurgled. He was lugging half his library with him. Even though he didn't really need the books, he had them all *in his head*. Even so: Better safe than sorry! Quickly through the Papendiek, where the Jews lived quietly and eagerly. Sometimes he had someone to carry his books. A student would do it, always for two semesters at a time. Because Lichtenberg didn't want to burden himself with their names—"my memory's full of all sorts of other things"—he always called them Müller. Sometimes Müller was short and squat, at other times he was angular and lanky. He stood at the garden gate, and waited for Lichtenberg to signal to him. Not having a watch, he often had to wait a long time. When Lichtenberg finally opened the front door, he would run up to him. This time Müller had brown rotted teeth and thick fair hair. Because everyone was always grabbing his hunchback, Lichtenberg grabbed at Müller's hair.

I just want to see how thick yours is, he said. I've lost most of mine!

Mine is the same as always, said Müller, relieving him of the books.

Everything with me is the same as always too, said Lichtenberg. Which means that everything is diseased!

When Müller spoke to him, he was chewing on his long churchwarden's clay pipe. I'm fogging myself up, he said. All right then, he said, let's go! and they headed down the Prinzenstrasse in the direction of the library. The fine weather, said Müller, has brought out all the pretty girls!

Is that right, said Lichtenberg, I never look!

Really young ones too, said Müller, fledglings!

I don't see any, said Lichtenberg.

Müller with his long pipe was walking right behind him. And so they trotted through Göttingen, where everyone knew them. They received many greetings. The library was a couple of streets away, "a crooked cat's leap." May I, said Müller, going on ahead. It's safer this way, then people will know the Professor's coming, and they won't run you down! Plus I'll keep the wind off you!

But there isn't any wind, said Lichtenberg.

No, but you never know.

Pedestrians looked up at them, and took in his hunchback. The women walked arm in arm, but so did the men as well. Once they had passed, they would turn round to view him from the back. Funny little mannikin reading books and trotting off to the theatre, to look for like-minded individuals that he could laugh with. Sometimes he thought: There's one! and beamed at him. But the other never once beamed back, and Lichtenberg would say: Please forgive me! He referred to himself as an *occasional* or *drawing room penseur*. He had written it down somewhere too, only he couldn't remember where it was now. He was convinced that the man and his soul both ceased at the point of death.

Do you mean altogether, asked Dr. Gatterer, and Lichtenberg replied: Altogether!

And what do you think will happen then?

Lichtenberg, bewigged, becaned, was walking along beside his friend, only at a lower altitude. They were talking about *that other*, meaning the soul! Lichtenberg had thought about it a lot, and was blinking in the sun. Then he shut his eyes and said: Nothing will happen then!

What do you mean, nothing at all?

Nothing at all!

That's what Lichtenberg said to anyone who wanted to hear it, and even to those who didn't. He encountered shock and indignation.

In the Spring, he dreamed of a woman whom he "first meant to draw to himself, then secure by means of his drollery." In the Summer, he dreamed of a different woman whom he . . . In the Autumn . . . In Winter! It finished with him clambering about on top of her. But in the meantime, he was giving a course on "various kinds of air, fire and electricity, including also magnetism." Then the subject was shooting. Lichtenberg leaned in a corner, and shot. In the process he so alarmed a student that his jaw dropped and he couldn't move it any more. Then experiments involving exploding gas. "I took the largest ox-bladder I could find in Göttingen, and filled it to capacity. The report was so huge that all the dogs in the parish as far down as the Pauliner Strasse, commenced to bark, and would not be pacified for hours." From then on, whenever there was banging in Göttingen, and someone was all of a heap, people said: Not to worry, it's just the Professor doing his shooting! (In their dialect, they said: shoo'in'.) Of course there was a bad smell now, and Lichtenberg said: It smells of students! His wig was powdered. When he had to splutter and sneeze, he called out: Powder, powder! Then he took his wig off, and beat it against the wall. As he climbed the steps, he called out: Slowly, slowly! I've got something in my brainbox that I mustn't lose! Once in the lecture room, he drew himself up to his full height and said: Here comes erudition!

Along with the streetlamps, the University had come to Göttingen, where it occupied the former riding school. The stablemaster was a member of the faculty. "The streetlamps," wrote Lichtenberg "create illumination outside. I try to do the same inside."

Before the room filled up in the morning, Lichtenberg liked to stick his head in the door. He wanted to see if the students were already in place. In fact, he was looking to see if the cleaning ladies were there and were getting to work. If they were there, he cried: At last! Then he walked up to them, and pinched the cheeks of the little ones. Nice and firm! he said. If they happened to be leaning against the wall or were even momentarily sitting down, he would pinch them on the upper arm and say: There too! If he found himself alone in a corner with one, he took her by the chin and turned her head around. He tried to kiss her on the mouth, but he couldn't reach. Then the cleaning lady would laugh, and he said: Ah well, never mind! and he went off to one of his three studies.

In the morning, rain or shine, his lecture room was always empty. There were only tables and chairs present. They were all scraped and gouged, "as if a hungry student had been nibbling at them." An hour later, and Lichtenberg was all spiffed up. He had washed out his eyes so as to be able to see. He had tipped rosewater over his collar, and not stinted! The room was full now. One might have expected him to be pleased, but was he pleased? Not a bit of it! When he asked himself what they had come for, he didn't think: So they can learn something from me! but: Because they want to stare at my hunchback uninterruptedly for a whole hour!

They talked about it as well. Some said: It keeps getting smaller! and others: No, bigger! Then they saw him sitting on the chair and said: How many have come to listen, and how many have come to look! Lichtenberg pretended not to hear. He was off inside his head. He asked Müller: Have you brought my books for me?

Yes, said Müller.

Unless I'm mistaken, said Lichtenberg, they weren't so heavy today! and Müller said: Oh, I thought they were as heavy as always! Thereupon Lichtenberg sighed and reached inside his coat, but there was nothing there and Müller said: Never mind! I thought not! And he went and sat down with the others. Because Lichtenberg was so short, he couldn't afford to sit. His day's work began.

He was now past thirty-five, and he was looking for . . . It could be a girl as well, she'd become a woman in due course anyway. Because he wanted not just to be better-looking, but younger as well, Lichtenberg claimed to be thirty-three.

Wasn't that vain of him?

Sometimes, as he once wrote, he wanted "to be done with the whole thing quicker." After his death, people realized that he had duped the world. "But that doesn't matter," he wrote, "it's used to it!"

He was wearing—let's be honest now!—his coat! He had brown stockings under it. His wig, which normally was matt, was shiny today. Wasn't he elegant? No more lying down now, not on a weekday! The students sat singly or in little clumps in the lecture room. When Lichtenberg noticed an unfamiliar face, he looked down at his feet. Sometimes he would get red splotches on his face, and he stumbled over his English.

"My poor spirit happens to have been poured into a miserable vessel," he wrote to Alessandro, Count Volta (1745–1827). Then he looked up the street again, to see if there wasn't maybe a pretty girl or a beautiful woman coming, who would fall in love with him, preferably before the break. But none was.

Later on, he went into his experimenting corner, where his equipment stood. There were dishes and jars and bottles and, hulking right in the middle, his electricity machine. Müller had to crank it, while little Lichtenberg explained it to his little ones. Sometimes he manipulated something that steamed and ponged and wanted to explode. Usually, though, it didn't, and everyone was disappointed. Suddenly he threw his hands up in the air and cried: I've got it! He thought he had stumbled across something big, at least the very edge of it, but it retreated from him, and once more he was all alone with his "idea that has shrivelled and gone cold." He forgot it again. Others came along, his own and other men's, "he stashed them all in his pocket." Then he went out in the garden.

That was where ideas were weighed, pros and cons. Lichtenberg sat down at the garden table, picked up his quill, and ordered an air pump, the first in Germany, from the English inventor, Edward Nairne (1726–1806). It would cost him over four hundred and twenty talers, more than a year's salary, but it was worth it. When visitors came, he called: What's keeping you? Come along, show yourselves! I've got something astonishing to show you! And he took his visitor by the sleeve, and hauled him into his experimenting corner, which was separated from the rest of the room by a black drape. He called it "my laboratory." Quick, he called, I want to show you something you've never seen before! And he led his visitor to his pride and joy, his air pump. He plucked the cover off it. It sparkled and gleamed like the open sea.

Well, he said, what do you say to that?

His friend—Blumenbach, as it might be, or Dr. Herschel—would have been walking for miles, or sitting on horseback or had come by stagecoach from Hanover. He was completely out of breath. He ran his fingertips over the expensive equipment, and Lichtenberg, who loved talking in English, asked: Isn't she a beauty? Then it was inspected and discussed from all sides. Dr. Volta, surgeon and physicist from Parma, visited him to have the pump explained to him, in French, because Lichtenberg's Italian wasn't up to it. He meant to learn, though, for his great trip to Rome. (He never made it to Rome.) Scarpa, de Luc, Chladni and Lessing, they too all gazed at the pump and stroked it with their fingers.

Careful, said Lichtenberg, it's a delicate thing! Let's not upset it!

When another piece of equipment—the "speaking machine, including description of its speaking parts"—was damaged on arrival, he was inconsolable. "The little fellow" wrote his teacher Abraham Gotthelf Kästner (1719–1800), "plunged out of the house and took the broken machine out of its box, like a father his drowned child from the stream." At night, when he finally lay down, he put the dead thing next to his double bed. He laid his trembling hand on it. Maybe he even cried.

And then?

Behind him in the lecture room was the slate blackboard, on which he could only manage to write along the very bottom edge. Sometimes he rested his head against it, then his collar was immediately besmirched, and everyone pointed at it.

Oh dear! said Lichtenberg, where does all that come from? and he quickly patted it clean again.

Sometimes he would write something on the board, as high as he could reach, and sometimes it would be wrong. For instance, instead of the formula he wanted to think about, he wrote down the name of a girl who happened to be on his mind. Of course his students then asked him what the girl's name was doing on the board. He said: It was a slip of the pen! and he wiped the girl away again. He wrote a fine hand, with very straight upper and lower extensions. As he wrote, he was at pains not to show the students his hunchback. God knows how he managed to write like that! When the lecture was over, and he was leaving the classroom, he sidled out, so that they didn't notice the hunchback so much. Once he was outside, everyone wondered whether he actually had one.

And what else?

His walk! As already mentioned, he could never have enough air. He clutched at his heart and cried: Where has it got to? Please overtake me, he said, I'm not in any hurry!

They called him "the little wheeze."

Ideas often came to him while he was walking, usually ideas about books. "A book," he wrote, "is a mirror. If a monkey looks into it . . . Oh no," he said, "we've already had that one!" Or: "Germany, where they teach you to turn up your nose, but not to blow it . . ." Often it was just a feeble little thing. But that too had to be committed to paper! Even that is a child of mine, he said, and I won't disown it! He was the only one who knew what might be made of it, and so he looked after it and tended it. As a "committed pedestrian," he always carried his jotter around with him. He hoped he would have an idea that he could manage to take home with him, because there he had a thick notebook that he had stitched together from lots of little ones, just waiting "for the thoughts of his life." The notebook was always waiting. When a sentence came to him on the Pauliner Strasse, he flopped down onto a bench, and examined it closely. If he liked it, he said: That's a keeper! and he started scribbling. "It's high time," he scribbled, "to grab hold of the world, in the form of a girl or a young woman, because otherwise it were all too easy to fall off it altogether!" Or: "The only manly attribute I have, decency unfortunately prevents me from displaying."

In the event that he had a companion with him on his walk through Göttingen — perhaps the globetrotting Georg Forster or Dr. Schlichtegroll — who wanted to stop with him, he often said: I just need to put something down on paper! Why don't you go on, I'll catch up! Then he wrote: "Our life is suspended between pleasure and pain! Sometimes it's a little closer to the former, sometimes the latter." Or: "Even the crawling of an insect helps me to answer questions about my destiny. Is that not curious in a professor of physics? Then, when I've drunk a glass of wine . . ." There was more he might have said, but he thought that was enough.

Göttingen was on the small side of metropolitan, consisting of three or four longish streets and twenty or thirty short cross streets. It was Lutheran, and contained eight parishes: St. Albani, St. Jakobi, St. Johannis, St. Marien, St. Crucis, St. Nicolai and the army one. Once he passed one of these churches in the company of the painter Chodowiecki (1726–1801). Lichtenberg told him behind which of them and at what depth—very deep!—he wanted to be buried. Chodowiecki said: I see! and Lichtenberg quickly changed the subject.

Anyway, Göttingen was situated in the "runnel of the Leine," as it was universally called. Everyone stared at him. Today, said one, he's got his long wig on, the one that's fraying!

Maybe he couldn't find the other one, said another.

He had it yesterday!

That wasn't yesterday, said a fourth, that was the day before yesterday!

Noon had rolled around. As Lichtenberg stepped into the kitchen, he unbuttoned his coat. He took off his wig, and tossed it at the hook. He missed, as he always did. So he cried: Missed! and seated himself at the table. In one corner of the kitchen hung the utensils, in another were the herbs. Lichtenberg sat down at the table, and scraped at the surface. He scraped cautiously, because not long ago he had caught a splinter from his scraping. He ate a plate of soup. If he was still hungry, he ate a second. At night, he ate five potatoes, an apple, and a crust of black bread. If the harvest had been good, he ate a crust of white. He referred to his cook as Bain-Marie, because she wasn't much given to washing. Sometimes she cooked him a piece of lean meat, sometimes a piece of fat. Lichtenberg waved it about in front of his nose, eyeing it suspiciously.

Couldn't you find anything else, he asked.

No.

Did you look?

No, she said. And she went into her room, and shut the door behind her. It was the time of the American War of Independence. The east coast of Australia had been discovered by Captain James Cook. England consoled herself for the loss of the United States by occupying India. Cook went on his third voyage, and met his death in Hawaii. Gluck sat in Vienna and composed, Haydn ditto. Lichtenberg, to whom no one paid any very great attention had now been alive for thirty-three years — thirty-five really. He had another twenty-two to go, but he wasn't to know that. Now he had finished his lunch. He poked around in his teeth with the toothpick he kept in his waistcoat pocket. What now? he asked himself, and went for a little lie-down on his sofa. If it wasn't too hot or too cold, he flung open the windows. Now he was gathering strength. If it was winter, there was snow in the air. Then Lichtenberg threw a blanket over his hunchback and looked up at the sky. Yes, there was something falling! He tried to forget all that was going on in his head, but it all went on just the same. Then he said: Well then, not today, it seems! and he got up, slipped into his soft shoes and ran out of the room. He didn't have quite so many books to carry now, but even so, even so! And then an idea wanted to come to him, but Lichtenberg wouldn't let it. He was thinking of a woman, or a girl! Müller and Meerbaum and von Amelung, all of them had one, and he didn't. He drew himself up on his lectern, as high as he possibly could.

Now then, he cried, what is Nature? and he stood before his little ones. He thought: How magnificent we are today! He didn't show his hunchback.

2.

*I*N WINTER, LICHTENBERG wore a woollen waist-coat and was very lonely. He had headaches all the time, and kept rubbing his skull. Everyone else was sitting in their rooms with their wives and families, watching the windows freeze over. Lichtenberg watched as well, and he began a scientific investigation of ice-flowers. He made some extraordinary discoveries that later all turned out to be wrong. All in all, though, it wasn't a bad time for him. A fire burned in his grate, and he wore thick socks. He spent hours staring at the glowing coals, thinking of a woman. When he had looked into the flames for long enough, he could find faces in them. To warm up his inner man, he brewed some punch. When he had had enough of looking at the faces, he started looking at the people that went with them: the father who had frittered everything away, the mother who had kept it all together, the brother and sister who had been so young at the time that he couldn't remember them any more, and who had long since *gone on*. Only in his head were they still all alive. Only when he was dead too would they all be *properly* dead. Well, it'll be a while till then, thought Lichtenberg, and took another sip. He kept it in his cheek, to make more of it. To his friends he wrote long winter letters, posing them the sort of riddles that life posed him, such as:

> "My first is not little,
> My second not hard,
> My all makes you hope,
> But don't trust too far!"

Sometimes he thought: You really ought to get out and about a bit, otherwise they'll forget you even exist! and he pulled on his red waistcoat. He put on his wig, and trotted off to a concert. There was more than just music on offer. There were pretty young ladies sitting there, maybe he would catch one? Lichtenberg went right up to them, but he didn't manage to catch any. They were only there for display purposes. The hall was very full. With his hunchback and his awful teeth, he didn't like to show himself. He went to the corner by the door, and walked up and down. When someone failed to notice him and walked into him, the fellow would just laugh at him, and say: Sorry, little man!

The pleasure's entirely mine, replied Lichtenberg.

As he feared he would be knocked over and trodden to death by his fellow-beings—his "life-fear"—he stood in a corner, and allowed the young ladies to file past him. Standing among them, with music in the offing, was enough to plunge him into a reverie. Good God, he thought, where have they all come from, these music-lovers? There were candles burning in the orchestra pit, just as in a funeral parlor. Lichtenberg sat down next to the tall doorway, he wasn't up to standing for that long. He pulled out his waste book, and wrote: "The critics would have us stick with Nature, and the authors read that. But after a while, they feel safer sticking with those authors who themselves once stuck with Nature." Then he put his notebook away again. The coats of the men had flapping tails that flared out from the waist. They were stiffened by the introduction of oilcloth, horsehair or paper. So that something of the shirt could also be seen, they were done up with a single button. The cuffs could not be too wide.

In the hall, people started to get impatient. Then everybody clapped, and the music began. Lichtenberg heard a piece by Handel, and then one by Rameau. He smiled to himself while they played. He had an affection for music, "which first exists beside us, then within us, but always a little higher, always over our heads." By the time he got home on his short legs, he had forgotten it again.

To him, Göttingen was "a dreadful hole that once you're in it, is hard to get out of." Even the air oppressed him, "both figuratively and literally." In the evenings, people stood outside their doors in the hope of maybe seeing some new face they hadn't seen before. Everyone knew everyone, and the boredom was killing. The man with the leopard would turn up at the weekend, but all too rarely! It didn't even have to be a leopard, a horse would have done just as well. Usually they came trotting over from Hanover, in all bright colors. When a circus rider came by with his stable lad, everyone thronged the streets. Even Lichtenberg wanted to see him, and why wouldn't he? He had bought himself an equestrian waistcoat to feel a little more involved. The horses, the great stallions especially, towered over him. He went up to the fence, because he didn't want to miss anything. The animal had a proud gait and carried itself very upright. Lichtenberg took out his pen and wrote: "With writing, if the little bit you do isn't eye-catching, at least try to express it in an eye-catching manner!" The people in front of him and beside him had hats on, and Lichtenberg didn't see much. So he turned round, and went back into the Gotmarstrasse. He couldn't watch any animal for very long, least of all any big animal. He didn't really want one. What he wanted was a woman!

Then, when he had been sitting all alone for some time, stroking one of his tables, he felt: Your place isn't in an empty room! That's unnatural! You should be among people! You should be with Gatterer and Schlichtegroll! and he accepted a supper invitation. That was generally on a weekend. Because everyone wanted to see his hunchback, he got lots of invitations. Maybe he would meet the young lady there who would take a shine to him! When he had his wig on, and set foot in the strange house, it was usually already dark. Lichtenberg was wearing his pink waistcoat, but it wasn't so conspicuous in the dark. Since lots of guests were expected, the front door had been left ajar. Lichtenberg went and stood in a corner, where he attracted less attention. There they all came one after the other. All of them bringing their wives with them, or their fiancées, who were younger than the wives. Lichtenberg tweaked at his wig, and looked up at them.

Why are you hiding, asked the lady of the house, taking him by the hand.

I'm not hiding, said Lichtenberg. I'm just small!

She led him to the table. They helped him up onto the children's high chair that was ready and waiting for him. Then they wedged a couple of cushions under him, so he could reach his little plate and his little glass. Now I'm almost on a level with the others, albeit artificially, he thought and looked along the line. He nodded to one or other of them, and laughed and ate and drank. He wanted to behave like everyone else, only he couldn't manage it. He pushed his plate away, and talked about this and that, for instance that "he'd seen a grave on his cheek today."

A grave?

Yes, said Lichtenberg, a grave! And now, he said, I'm working on electricity.

On what?

Quite right, cried Lichtenberg, and attempted from up on his high chair to explain to the other guests, Gatterer, Schlichtegroll and so forth, the nature of electricity, which he himself didn't understand. He didn't believe in a single big experiment, he said, he believed in lots of little ones, "that I can perform in my own kitchen at home."

In your kitchen, chorused everyone, and Lichtenberg said: Yes of course, in my kitchen!

The times were, like all times, extraordinary. Many discoveries were made. Now it was the presence of electricity in nature, both living and dead. It was demonstrated in dogs, cats and other hirsute animals. Lichtenberg sat on his cushions. He had his legs apart. It wasn't elegant, but . . . He had his wig on, and was tweaking at it. On account of the many scientific expressions he was using that evening, they didn't understand what he was saying. Before long, no one was listening to him any more. Everyone had had a few, and now they wanted to talk. Lichtenberg, on his high chair, was talking less and less. Then he had himself lifted down, and he went next door, where he had neither to talk nor to listen. The others all left their empty plates and came too. The ladies detached themselves from the gentlemen, and each formed little groups. They reseated themselves. The gentlemen had taken out their long pipes and jammed them between their teeth. Now smoke was coming out of them. Everyone was stretching their legs and desired, like everything else in the world, to be left in peace. Lichtenberg walked amongst them and looked at them. Well, he thought, so that's what they're like! Then he'd seen enough of the men, and he went over to the ladies. They were all drinking tea. Oh, Lichtenberg sighed, and he wanted to get back to the gentlemen quickly, but the ladies held on to him and said: Won't you stay with us for a little quarter of an hour! Then he had his toothpick between his dreadful teeth, and went back and forth between the two rooms. He went into a corner, pulled out his notebook and wrote: "A little quarter of an hour is longer than a quarter of an hour!" When he had drunk his coffee, something strange happened. He noticed that he twitched at certain sounds before the sound was even heard. "We therefore hear with other organs than our ears," he wrote, "we have an inner hearing. When we expect to hear something, we duly hear it!"

Once a week, in the warm weather, he slipped into his green coat and went bowling. When two skittles collided with each other, he exclaimed: Pardee! In the event of his own colliding with a pretty girl, he had his pink waistcoat on. When none had come for a long time, he took it off again. Later on, the sky grew dark. His friends—"Friends?"—were in the garden, candles had been lit. The bowling balls he had to sling were too heavy for him. Too heavy? he said, they're perfect! Then he cried: All nine! and he began to sweat.

Look at it pouring off you, cried his friends.

Yes, he said, it's warm work!

Wouldn't you rather sit and watch?

No, cried Lichtenberg, I want to bowl too!

What soft air! What summer nights! It was all dark around Lichtenberg now. The trees were still fragrant from the sunshine, especially the limes. His friends played on by candlelight, they could hardly see anything. Lichtenberg lacked the strength, his shots didn't have any impetus. Well, he thought, perhaps it'll stimulate me! Perhaps I'll grow a bit, and next week I'll fare better!

What are you talking about, they asked him, and Lichtenberg said: Maybe I was just composing some verses! Then it was midnight, and the moon shone down upon them in its endless deceitfulness. At home on his scribbling table, everything was silent and dark. Lichtenberg had wanted to write down one more thing, but then he forgot. Pity, he thought, now it won't come back! I wonder where it went?

He didn't go out much in those days, he preferred to have people come to him. There would suddenly be someone at the door, who had forgotten to announce his visit. Lichtenberg surveyed himself, and saw that his stocking was torn. That's not right, he thought, I'll have to stay in my room! Sometimes he found a spare stocking and slipped it on, but his mood wasn't improved. Then he flung the window open, and shouted for the man with the English organ. He wore an earring, and doffed his cap to Lichtenberg. All his tunes were sad. All except the "Old Dessauer," at which Lichtenberg would perk up again.

He even went to parties and dances, because women would come. The beautiful yellow villa in the Kurze Geismarstrasse, where the ball was taking place, was all lit up, you could see there was something going on there. When you got a little nearer, you could hear it too. Even the rooms that didn't have dancing in them were lit up. Everything was magnificent. And there, into the midst of that magnificence, went Lichtenberg! Because Göttingen had seen all his coats, he had wrapped a silver cloth round his neck. He waited till the anteroom was empty, then he quickly stepped inside. Because he couldn't dance, he stood in a corner. Then, with his hunchback always following him, he went from room to room. In the first of them, the musicians, a trio, had set up. They were on loan from Hanover, no party was complete without them. They were dressed like footmen, all identically. Their wigs were white with powder. Their coats were buttoned up at the top, and then slashed open over chest and belly. The sleeves went down to the elbows, no further. Under their breeches, they wore silk stockings that they often tugged at. Completely expressionless, they began fiddling away. Lichtenberg stood in a corner and listened. "As agreeable as music is to the ear," he wrote later, "so disagreeable it is when people talk during it!"

But the ladies!

The ladies laughed and rapped their hands with their fans. Lichtenberg sat with the ladies who didn't have a dancing partner. They didn't mind him being there. They perched on their little stools, felt bored, and weren't allowed to show it. Lichtenberg held a glass in his hand, from time to time he took a sip from it. Behind him were three young Englishmen, whom he was supposed to be teaching German. They stepped up to him.

German is a very difficult language, said one.

Oh, exclaimed Lichtenberg, won't you leave me alone!

What did he say, they asked one another.

Lichtenberg put his arms out, and pushed the young men away. One of them made a joke. He asked why he wasn't dancing, and Lichtenberg shrugged his shoulders and said mysteriously: Who knows! Then another one asked: If you're not dancing, what are you doing in this room, in this house, in this world? and Lichtenberg replied: I'm spending the best years of my life taming young Englishmen! Thereupon he emptied his glass. With the wine now flowing not just in bottles and decanters, but in his veins, he went back to the Gotmarstrasse, to his cold, empty double bed, which was a little hollowed out in the spot where his hunchback rested.

3.

PROFESSOR KÄSTNER (1719–1800) liked to stand by the window. He was twenty-three years older than Lichtenberg, and of course much, much taller. There are pictures of him too. He had a well-tended wig, powdered white and presumably scented as well. Only the edges of his large ears are visible. "Ears, that," as Lichtenberg wrote in his wastebook, "one would like to trim with a pair of scissors!" His coat was a scholar's coat in subfusc. A silk stock bubbled up around his throat. Dr. Kästner suffered from swollen legs, because he spent so much time sitting down. So that nothing hampered his speech, he liked to leave all his buttons undone. He was a member of the same faculty as Lichtenberg, only one or two grades higher. He was Lichtenberg's academic mentor, and he sometimes waved to him with one finger. That meant: I want to see you now, little man!

"Everything I want to be, he already is," Lichtenberg wrote to Lavater, "and everything I want to do, he has already done!" Lichtenberg was always deferential to him. He held the door open for him.

How extraordinarily amiable of you, to seek me out in my scholarly abode, he said as he walked in.

What other option do I have, seeing as you've been pestering me for months with invitations, said Professor Kästner. It's impossible to cross the street without getting an invitation from you. Have you at least got a chair for me?

Even now flying in, cried Lichtenberg, grappling with a padded armchair.

Well, exert yourself, said Professor Kästner. I really don't want to break anything here, having caught a stomach distemper the last time, I mean, he said, break an arm or a leg. So careful how you put your stool down, he said, and then I can listen to you, in case you have anything to say to me! Then Kästner pointed at Schlichtegroll and Gatterer and said: Ha, colleagues! Fellow-trenchermen, unless I'm mistaken, he said, and the pair of them replied: Salve, magister!

Well now, said Professor Kästner, I can't stay long, but seeing as you've prepared some little snack . . . I can smell it already! I trust you didn't stick it on the hob yourself, but left it to some qualified person to prepare! What have you got in there, asked Professor Kästner, who, like all men of learning, had a greedy sensual nature, and Lichtenberg said:

A little soup, mon cher maître, a little soup!

To be served piping hot, I trust.

Oh, piping!

And is it too much to hope that you might have dropped a piece of tenderloin in it?

Absolutely, said Lichtenberg. Plop!

Which you won't bring to table, as last time, half raw? I only need to think of it, and I feel my distemper upon me again, said Professor Kästner.

Today, said Lichtenberg, she's cooked it through. She swore to me she has!

Well, let's hope so, said Professor Kästner, at last sitting down. Whereupon the others sat down too. The conversation abated.

The weather, volunteered Dr. Schlichtegroll abruptly, it's as though it's cut out of a book!

Except for the wind, said Dr. Gatterer, the wind!

Oh, is it windy, asked Lichtenberg, turning towards the window. Windy or not, said Professor Kästner, completely otiose! The whole conversation thus far, completely otiose! I suggest you pick it up wherever you were when I interrupted you!

And where were we, asked Gatterer.

His trip to London, said Schlichtegroll. Well then, said Professor Kästner, tell us what you saw! Where were you again . . .

In England, said Lichtenberg.

And what did you do there, asked Professor Kästner, and for the two thousandth time Lichtenberg told how he'd spent two weeks being driven about in Lord Boston's chaise in the biggest . . .

and most expensive, threw in Professor Kästner.

. . . city in the world. Had it not been for His Lordship and his chaise, he would have had to spend the whole time in his digs, staring at the clouds. I would have liked, said Lichtenberg, to stay in London, instead of withering away here, but it wasn't possible. I should have had to buy myself a completely new life in London, which would have far exceeded my resources.

Don't you have any friends there, asked Professor Kästner.

Indeed I do, very distinguished people among them, like Lord Marchmont, who spent seventeen minutes conversing with me in full view of the Houses of Parliament, and visited me the following day and told me . . . Well, said Lichtenberg, never mind what he told me! And he had spoken with Lord Boston too. Who is, said Lichtenberg, an implacable devotee of mathematics. He is much taken with Göttingen and with the Germans. It surprises him that there is no description of Göttingen in English. How avidly the ladies in London drawing rooms would read such a thing, over their tea or their punch!

Apropos punch, said Professor Kästner, are we not your guests?

Forgive me my absent-mindedness, though it's quite unpardonable, cried Lichtenberg, and went and fetched bottles and glasses.

Do you still live alone, Professor Kästner asked him.

Yes, said Lichtenberg, alone with my books! They're the best company a man could wish for!

So you require rest and solitude?

I can't afford all this travel! I sit in my little room, and acquire culture at a remove, said Lichtenberg.

So do we, cried Dr. Gatterer and Dr. Schlichtegroll.

So, asked Professor Kästner, there is no bride in the picture? and Lichtenberg replied: Not in this picture!

Well, a man doesn't need a wife to get through life, said Professor Kästner, and Lichtenberg said: Yes, but it shows!

Where in particular do you think it shows?

Above all in the soul.

Then they touched glasses and drank and sat around some more. In the kitchen, the meat was sizzling away. Potatoes were boiling in the big saucepan next to it. Then Lichtenberg said: Of course! and suddenly sprang up and went upstairs, because that was where the smallest room in the house always was in those days. Dr. Kästner and Gatterer and Schlichtegroll watched him go. A longer conversation followed. Gatterer was the first to speak.

Gatterer: So he's off to the privy, and left us to ourselves!

Professor Kästner (walking about, scanning the room for something to smoke): Well, really! Nothing! Nothing! Nothing!

Schlichtegroll: After my coachman and my end
                   Stole me from your sight, my friends . . .

Gatterer: Does he still scribble?

Professor Kästner: Yes, in his wastebook!

Schlichtegroll: He says it makes the world more palatable!

Gatterer: With those short legs of his, he's surely not long for the world?

Professor Kästner: Whenever he stops, it's so that he can think of something!

Schlichtegroll: Yes, mainly about air!

Gatterer: And don't forget the weight of the head that's tee-tering on top!

Schlichtegroll: His arms go down to his knees! I won't name the other animal to which that applies!

Professor Kästner: You ask yourself: Was that all? when he walks by.

Schlichtegroll: Yes, but he's clever!

Professor Kästner: You can tell he's clever and witty just from looking at him, just as you can look at a greyhound and tell he's fast!

Schlichtegroll: Unfortunately, his little legs don't carry him as easily as they should such a young man! One day . . .

Gatterer: Then he'll live on in our memory, getting smaller and smaller.

Schlichtegroll: You think so? Even smaller?

Professor Kästner: If he really dies, do you think he'll leave us anything in his will?

Schlichtegroll (reckoning on his fingers): His rented apartments with his Bain-Marie, his barometer and the half dozen maps he'd like to put up on the wall. But he can't reach high enough!

Gatterer: Why does he tell us his thoughts as if they were those of some stranger?

Professor Kästner: There are some people who can't get enough of the *first* person, but *he* can't get enough of the *third*!

Gatterer: He's a ponderer and an introspective, but may yet become Professor philosophiae extraordinariae. He thinks about everything, and writes down his thoughts in his barely legible script. He is interested in the most abstruse questions . . .

Professor Kästner: What are they?

Gatterer: Those that have occupied him all his life! Others ask themselves: What is in my head? but he asks himself: What is in my hunchback?

Schlichtegroll: What do you mean? Is there something in it?

Gatterer: If what he told me is true, then in London, which he seems to know like his own herb garden . . .

Professor Kästner: Do you think he ever was in London? I can't quite bring myself to believe it!

Schlichtegroll: The eyes were popping out of his head! His scribbling fingers couldn't keep up with what he saw all around him.

Gatterer: In London, he met a Lord, who, after the merest of acquaintance, took him aside . . .

Professor Kästner: Pretty morals! After such a brief acquaintance!

Schlichtegroll: He records everything, simply everything! The launching of a frigate on the Thames, a water-spout, a curious cloud formation, everything! These are, he says, the objects of our existence, and we should try to hold on to them! In the same way as, in the person of some girl . . .

Professor Kästner: Some what?

Schlichtegroll: . . . some girl or young friend or family, we hold on to the world, so as not to slip off it.

Gatterer: Anyway, the young Lord took him aside and asked him if he might go up to his room with him for five or ten minutes, for a certain purpose. Our hunchbacked friend is said to have been somewhat taken aback, haha, but as he was a gentleman of high birth, he obliged him. Once there, they are said to have . . .

Schlichtegroll: Allow me to interpose another story, very briefly . . . The great traveller Forster called on him in London, and our little friend was glad to lay his hand in that of Forster's, who had just returned from the other side of the world. Lichtenberg took him aside and asked him whether he, the toad, could survive a voyage round the world, if he wrapped up warmly. Thereupon Forster turned him this way and that and finally said: Why not? But nothing came of it. But I've interrupted you. Please!

Professor Kästner: Don't be a frog and tell us what the milord said to him when they were sitting on the sofa together.

Gatterer: Well, first of all he didn't say anything, and then after they'd spent quite a while on his little bed, in his little bedroom, sitting side by side . . .

Schlichtegroll: Sitting? Not lying?

Gatterer: . . . sweating in silence, His Lordship suddenly moved right up close to him and said he had a request to make. And then he made it. He asked if the toad would be good enough to take off his shirt, and let him touch his hunchback very quickly. Whereupon, after fussing and faffing for a while, our friend took his shirt off and let him.

Schlichtegroll: And what was it like?

Gatterer: Just like any other hunchback!

Professor Kästner: Just as I always say. He's the most imaginative of our scholars!

Gatterer: And the most scholarly of our jokers!

Professor Kästner (looking around): And where is he now?

Schlichtegroll (reciting):   In the wide and windy spaces —
                              Because his pills are highly
                                  efficacious!

Professor Kästner: I see!

Gatterer: He's often tired.

Schlichtegroll: The little sleep that is but a foretaste of the great sleep to come!

Gatterer: He has beautiful eyes, even though he may not see very much with them.

Professor Kästner: And beautiful adjectives, like *well-grown, grey-materialist* and *mild-eyed*.

Schlichtegroll: Silentium! He approacheth!

Lichtenberg returned from the other end of his apartment, from the back of beyond.

Well, said Schlichtegroll, and have you substantially enriched the world?

I looked in on the kitchen on my way back, said Lichtenberg. The souping hour is at hand. It's already on the table. The plates are ready too. So, if I may. But please be careful, my dear friends, the stairs!

What are you trying to tell us, asked Professor Kästner, getting to his feet.

I was trying to tell you not to take them head first, said Lichtenberg, though that may be hard as well.

4.

*S*HORTLY THEREAFTER, Lichtenberg wrote a letter—still preserved—to his schoolfriend, the pastor Gottfried Hieronymus Amelung (1742–1800). "Just imagine," he wrote, "something has happened, all of a sudden! I've met a girl, a girl, a girl, a girl!—the daughter of someone in the town. [Here he was lying through his teeth, she wasn't a burgher's daughter at all, she was way below!] She is thirteen, and, I have to say, beautiful. I have never seen such a picture of beauty and gentleness. She was in a group of five or six others, doing what children do here, selling flowers up on the wall to passersby. She held out a bunch to me, which I bought on the spot. I had three young Englishmen with me, who had lodgings in the next house to mine. God almighty, one of them said, what a handsome girl! Knowing what a city of the plain this is here, I thought to rescue this excellent creature from such trade. So I took her aside, and asked her to call on me at home. She said she didn't go to some fellow's rooms. But when I explained that I was a professor, and the author of fourteen books, she came the following afternoon, with her mother. And now she wants to give up her florist's trade."

From that day forth, Maria Dorothea Stechard, known as *the little Stechardess*, lived with the hunchback on the first floor on the Gotmarstrasse, first as his pupil and housekeeper, then as his lover, round the back of the house, for discretion's sake. That was a condition the mother had insisted on, no one was to know. [Ridiculous, the next day, everyone knew!] They never exchanged any letters. It went on for some time, until . . .

5.

*A*T THAT POINT, IT WAS springtime, Lichtenberg said: Oh! The two of them were getting acquainted. Lichtenberg took a deep breath and thought: Well, who would have thought it!

His friends, for example, Friedrich Wilhelm Herschel (1738–1822), astronomer, sometimes visited him. Herschel looked at his books, and said: Aha, so you've got that one as well! He had just developed the reflector telescope, with which he would discover the planet Uranus. Others discovered air pressure and the circulation of the blood. They wrote long letters to Lichtenberg. Some of them they dated and sealed in envelopes, others they even forgot to seal. Lichtenberg asked them not to write so frequently. "In addition to my scientific work," he wrote, "there is some other business which has arisen to preoccupy me!"

The little fellow! Well, well! Whatever could he mean?

Lichtenberg stood by his window and thought: I'm busy! And all he was doing was trotting across his room, and thinking incessantly of her. It was the first time he wasn't absolutely alone with his acids and his alkalis—Bain-Marie called them fluids. A girl had "crawled into him, and was spreading out." Overnight, she stopped selling flowers. She began to distance herself from her little friends.

Wonder why, the people asked.

Maybe she has something better in mind, something involving him!

Anyway, she spent a lot of time sitting around at home. Some of it she was knitting. Next to her sat her mother, telling her about men. After every sentence her mother said, she said: I see! Her father liked to take a dram or two. The little Stechardess had the window open that faced the rear courtyard, so that no one could see her from the street. But she was there all the same, and how!

She must be bored, said the people when they walked past her house and didn't see her. Or could she be ill?

Just as the sun was going down, the child could be seen like a shadow going about the garden. She had on new shoes and a new dress. You could tell that from the way she walked.

Wonder who gave her those, someone asked.

And what, someone else asked, did she give him in return?

Did she give him something in return?

Must have, said someone else.

Lichtenberg had been Titular Professor of Philosophy at Göttingen for two years now, and people greeted him in the street. He always greeted them back. He was made to sit down a lot, and allow people to sketch him. For posterity, he thought, but that butters no parsnips! Sometimes he drew himself. As he couldn't take himself seriously, they were always caricatures. His writings and all-round smorgasbord made him celebrated far beyond the confines of Göttingen.

In the evening, he stood by the window, waiting for the darkness to creep up the Mühlenstrasse. Then he put on his wig and went over to see her. Since no one saw him coming, they said he walked "through the air." Be that as it may, suddenly he was standing knocking on the door. Her father, who was apt to be drunk, opened the door and shouted: Is anyone there? But of course it was "our little cripplet," as her mother affectionately called him. He was no longer dressed like a scholar, but like a little dandy. He didn't even notice though, he was thinking: Like a gentleman! At the front and back of his collar, a fine linen shirt escaped. His wig was brand new. He said a couple of pleasantries to the father, and walked past him into the house. Then there were other voices to be heard, three or four, children for the most part. People were watching from the surrounding windows. When they'd spent long enough watching, they forgot about the visitor, and shut the windows again. Later on, they blew out their candles. Towards midnight, the little manikin was back on the street, setting off on its little legs. If it was a fine night, he would walk. At home, he sat down at his table, and noted: "Oh, what a sad amour it is, when after all that waiting around, a man takes to his bed alone! The first time the couple lie down together will be in the grave, and I can see us ending like that!" If it was raining, he grabbed the old man and shoved him out the door to find him a cab. He was quite professorial about that, and appeared to have grown a little. When it had got light and then dark again, he was back. He was wearing a different coat and a different wig. Look how vain I'm getting in my middle years, he thought to himself. Once, he had himself driven in a cab to her house, with a big parcel. When the coachman made to help him, he said: Leave it! I can manage! He could barely carry it. The coachman asked: What have you got in there? and Lichtenberg said: A present!

For your honeylove, asked the coachman, who liked poking fun at him.

That's none of your business, said Lichtenberg! Anyway, it's for her parents!

Then he pushed the package in front of him into the house, calling: Look out, here comes something! The door fell shut behind him, nothing further could be seen. Some of the neighbors wanted to see Lichtenberg come out again, and they almost fell asleep waiting. Before he went to bed himself, he wrote: "The girl is marvellous! She just requires a different setting!" In the following nights, it was the same, only Lichtenberg wasn't wearing silver buttons on his coat, but gilt ones, which, as people said, "must have cost him a fortune." Then there was one night in particular, such as Göttingen had rarely experienced. There was a lot of noise and rummaging about in the Stechardess's house. Hours later, Lichtenberg stepped out with the girl, and the door was bolted behind them. The coach had been left waiting for hours, and was still there. The Stechardess climbed into it with the little man, and they drove off.

Curious, people said the next day, first she's obdurate for weeks, and now she's suddenly disappeared! Where has she got to, they asked.

One mild spring night, "brutal, like all beautiful women, even if they are still children," she had moved into the house "of the hunchback."

And what are they doing there, people asked one another.

What do you think they're doing, said one person, they're making gogglemosh!

Certainly, no one had seen them arrive in the Gotmarstrasse. But a few had heard them. When they saw the cripple, they said: Lucky so and so! It must be the hunchback that does it! But what will he do with that little slip of a thing? They would have pointed at them with their fingers if they'd seen them. But they didn't show themselves. They saw the cripple very rarely, and the girl not at all.

They must, they said, have crept into his house, and they walked up and down in front of it. If they hadn't been certain they were inside, they would have said the place is deserted. But from time to time they heard a sound. Sometimes a book fell to the floor, or something was knocked over. Was he really all alone with his books, like he was before? Sometimes he pulled his wig further into his face, and left the house by the back door. And then he came back with a big box. More sweeties for her?

Yes, nor was that all!

His so-called friends came and sniffed around. They were nicely done up, and all wearing new wigs. Sometimes they came through the front door, sometimes via the garden.

They didn't go in for any sort of preamble, they just called out: It's all right, we know everything! They had heard the Stechardess or seen her standing in the window. But that wasn't enough for them. They wanted to be absolutely certain, and they came knocking on the door. When Lichtenberg heard them knocking, he said: Excuse me! and he pushed the child into her little bedroom. Stay here, he said and locked the door behind him. There was another knock, and they entered, one by one, at intervals. Dr. Schlichtegroll had been at the bottle. You could smell it on him too. He was the first. Yes, he said, it's me! He peered into first one corner, then another, and asked: Have you got anyone here with you?

Here with me, asked Lichtenberg, who do you mean?

A person! There are noises!

No noises, said Lichtenberg, I'm all alone!

Dr. Schlichtegroll shook his drinker's head, and accepted a glass. Curious, when I've heard the noises so clearly, he said. He looked on the floor and in the air and even under the desk. Then he emptied his glass and left, and Lichtenberg ran to the door and said to the Stechardess: You can come out now! He's gone! But already there was the next visitor standing there, sniffing, Dr. Gatterer, for example. He looked in all the rooms and asked: What about here? Or here? He looked everywhere.

That's a store cupboard, said Lichtenberg.

And what's stored in there?

Whatever's in there, said Lichtenberg, and Dr. Gatterer said: I can smell young female flesh!

Young female flesh, what nonsense, said Lichtenberg, no one's stored in there, and Dr. Gatterer, having pressed his ears to all the doors, said: Curious, I was convinced you had someone in here with you!

Oh, who would I have in here with me, said Lichtenberg, and Dr. Gatterer said: I don't know, but I'm going to find out!

Then he took his professor's hat, and he left. Lichtenberg went: Phew! and was going to get the girl out again, but . . .

The third visitor, with his old man's gait, was Professor Kästner. He was breathing hard, cried: Sit down, sit down! and pulled a chair over to the wall. From there he could see all three rooms. His eye ranged from one corner to the next. I know you've got someone here with you, you so-called scholar, he said. There's no sense in trying to keep it a secret from me! I even know who it is!

Do you indeed, said Lichtenberg, in that case you know more than I do. Then, to distract him, he went over to one of his three desks, and scribbled something. He saw his shadow on the wall, and what he scribbled was: "Each time he picks up his pen, his own shadow laughs at him!"

What's that you're writing, asked Professor Kästner, peering at the paper over his shoulder.

Words, said Lichtenberg, as always.

Is it something important?

As usual!

And what about over there, said Professor Kästner, pointing at various doors, who's in there?

The same thing as everywhere else, replied Lichtenberg, nothing in other words!

Well all right, said Professor Kästner, but I'll be back. And he took himself home for now.

When Lichtenberg went into town during this period, he always walked very fast. They won't notice, he thought, I'll slip right under them! The people of Göttingen wore tight trousers and fairly flat hats. The eyes popped out of their heads, and they stared after him. What a dwarf! they said. Sometimes, at nightfall, they wanted to know for certain, and they slunk in front of his house. They stood under his drawing room window, and stared up. They never managed to catch sight of the girl. Curious, they said, and went home again. But even when they were just sitting around in their homes, they still weren't done with him. Then they would be talking about him and the Stechardess, the "beautiful child" that ate and drank and apparently *lived* with him.

You mean not only in the same house, but in the same room, asked one of them.

In the same room!

But not in the same bed!

In the same bed!

But is that allowed? I say, is that allowed?

They were all full of questions. They wanted to know how and when and how often she came to him. Where he *put her* during the day, because she was never spotted outside. Where, they asked, does he put her then?

In fact, Lichtenberg didn't put her anywhere. She stayed of her own accord. She propped her arms on the backs of chairs, and looked at everything in his beautiful scholar's suite of rooms in the Gotmarstrasse: the bookcases overflowing with books, the writing-desks, the paintings on the walls. But because he had forbidden it, she did not go to the window. First she stood in one corner, then another. When she dropped a stitch—she knitted as well!—he was able to help her out. He had moved into the library, to give her a room for herself. Lichtenberg had the one that smelled of tobacco, and of wine in the evenings. Here he would sit or stand by the window overlooking the street, and ask himself if he shouldn't just put his arm around her shoulders. Maybe I should, he thought, but not yet! It will just frighten her off!

He always sat in the "deep corner" now, reading or writing. She was next door with Bain-Marie, who didn't talk to her much. When he had once talked to her father and mother about his, the little cripple's, feelings, he noted: "I can't blame a girl for not abiding by the wishes of her parents in the choice of a lover. Is she to give something she has so often studied in the mirror, and scrubbed and polished, that has for so long been her only care, is she to give that to somebody she might not like, the sight of whom she might even hate?"

Such beautiful days they were, after all it was July! The Stechardess wore her light shoes, and went all over the flat. The doors were all open. She looked inside the cupboards. She knew what was in all of them. In the morning, when Lichtenberg was giving a lecture in the big room on the other side of the corridor, she heard the boom of his voice. Strange that such a little man should have such a big voice, she thought, going from one room to the next. Then she looked at herself in the mirror, and the sight made her rejoice. When she heard Lichtenberg come back from his lecture, she went to her room. There he could hear her breathe. Aha, he thought, she is with my books, at least they'll excite her! When the sun shone into the room, the books smelled differently from the way they did at night. She laid her hands on them, they were nice and warm. When the sun shone in his face, she drew the curtain, and he said: Thank you! Then he walked around her, sighing. When it was quiet and dark outside, the Stechardess heard him sighing at his desk. Sometimes he ran out of the house, and returned with a bunch of flowers for her, which he hid behind his back. Later they would go in a vase. Then the flowers would stand on her table for a long time. When she passed them she would smile. Sometimes his friend Lessing would come. He liked to look at this or that, for instance the leaf electroscope: Two thin sheets of metal were stuck to a brass rod by means of a little eggwhite or earwax, and parted when an electric current was passed through them.

Well, asked Lichtenberg, what do you say?

Nice, said Lessing, very nice!

Then, without the Stechardess, whom he had hidden in her room, they ate a beef soup together, and then Lessing went on his way. The Stechardess didn't come out until Lichtenberg went and got her, and then he carried on writing and calculating in his study. Often he had strange thoughts. "We should," he wrote, "encounter extraordinary people if the extensive parts of the globe that are currently seas were to become inhabited, and if, in a few thousand years' time, our lands and our seas were to change places. Completely new morals would have come into being, which would cause us to shake our heads." Such were his thoughts.

At table, over cutting and stirring and spooning, they next saw each other. Lichtenberg suffered the Stechardess to sit with him. Both had their hands in their laps, and didn't touch one another. Often there were long pauses in their conversation. To entertain her, he would often set her riddles.

A thing, he asked her, of whose nose and head we see little and whose eyes and ears nothing at all. What is it?

The Stechardess had her hands lying on her knees. She was too shy to think. She didn't know the answer. Lichtenberg, his hunchback behind him, said: Our own body!

Our own body, she asked in alarm. Then she said: Oh, I see!

Darkness had fallen, "yet another one," said Lichtenberg. He rolled up his napkin. The child thanked him for her food and drink, and then she ran off into her little room. He said: Ah yes! and then he walked up and down a little. He wanted to follow her to her room, and went up to the door. He already had his hand poised to knock, but didn't want to frighten her by appearing suddenly in the doorway like that. So he crept back to his apparatuses and sat down with them. There he was among friends. To the right was the Leyden Jar, and to the left Volta's audiometer. ("On his latest visit, I saw that the handsome Italian also knows something of the electricity of young women.") Lichtenberg put his hands to his head, because, "by pressing on a certain spot, it is possible to make a headache better." Yes, he had a headache again!

At night, there was silence in the Gotmarstrasse, and Lichtenberg didn't clap eyes on the Stechardess. Either she was at her mother's, or she had bolted the door of her room. Sometimes he could hear her sleeping. Sometimes she lit a candle, and appeared to be sitting in a corner. Or he pictured her in front of the mirror. He wanted to write something about his desire, and the pen was already in his hand to do so, but he couldn't think of anything. Maybe tomorrow, he thought, and clapped his wastebook shut again. Then he went over to his mountains of books, "over which," he once wrote, "I shall have to climb many times." He scratched his hump, the one at the back and the one at the front. He told himself: Mind you don't scare off the child! She'll come by and by, all in her own sweet time!

He was referring to her love.

Lichtenberg was now thirty-five, not thirty-three, as he would have people believe. He liked pulling the wool over their eyes in other ways too. "The greater part," he wrote, "of what I commit to paper is untrue, and the best of it is nonsense!" He often claimed to have been up all night writing, whereas in fact he had been sleeping, "like a bear." Or he attributed some unsuccessful piece of work to the authorship of a friend. When he was lying, he said: It's wrong to do that, and he started to sweat. When he was dry again, he lied some more. At night he often stood in front of her door, pressing an ear to it. He wanted to hear her breathing. Every sound that reached him, he would match up with some movement on her part. Because she wore straw-soled shoes, he could hardly hear her. Her bonnet was green and laced under the chin. Her chin was white and soft, and he would have loved to stroke it. Her skirts were black and dark-green, and reached almost down to the floor. That's how I'll picture her to myself, thought Lichtenberg, when she's booted out of my life again.

For a long time, he could hardly credit that the beautiful girl had moved in with him. He trotted around her a lot, and called her "my dear child." That always scared her, and she would run and stand in a corner.

More fine days followed, "they were what the year had purposed." Lichtenberg had a piece of equipment that could gauge the specific weight of fluids. It was kept in a velvet-lined box, and was called an areometer. Lichtenberg trotted back and forth in front of it. How restless I've become since knowing her, he thought. But he didn't say: It's the fault of that girl! he said: I blame the air in Göttingen! After a day spent thinking about the Stechardess, he said to himself: You've dreamed away the day! And in the morning he wrote in his wastebook: "Wasted another day dreaming!" He stepped up to his mirror, and dolled himself up. It was laughable, of course, but never mind, never mind! He patted powder in his face, and put his wig on. Sometimes he pulled it down over his ears, sometimes . . . Then it was once more time for lunch, which Bain-Marie brought in from the kitchen. As she was about to leave, he plucked her by the sleeve, and pulled her towards him. He straightened himself up as far as he could, and said: Now listen! Then he dug around in his pockets, and pulled out a sixpenny piece. He gave her instructions, "relating to the child that has joined our household."

Bain-Marie pocketed the sixpence, and asked him whether she was now expected "to feed her as well."

Yes, her as well, he said.

And how long do I have to go on feeding her for, asked Bain-Marie, and Lichtenberg said: She won't want to stay long before she moves on! So make some tea, and don't ask too many questions! Put the tea on the tray, nicely in the middle. Then I'll call you!

It was still light outside the window, even though the sun had already gone, "half-bright," as Lichtenberg once called it. While eating, he sometimes—"unintentionally"?—brushed the arm of the Stechardess with his fingertips. He hurriedly withdrew his hand, but the girl hadn't even noticed. They were shy of each other, and didn't talk much. Sometimes he said: A fine day! and she said: Yes, that's true!

He walked around her a lot, and wanted very much to touch her. Because that was not allowed, he would have liked to have long witty conversations with her instead, but he couldn't think of anything to say when she was so close to him. It was all he could do to look out of the window and say: Hm, dusk! The Stechardess wanted to nod by way of reply, but she didn't nod. That discouraged him from saying anything else. It had gotten dark outside now. He fetched a spill, and lit a few candles. They flickered a bit. Bain-Marie was creeping around some distant corner of the room. Because the Stechardess didn't want anything else to eat or drink, and also didn't want to speak, he sent her back to her room. Lie down and shut your eyes, I'll just be next door, he said, and he went into his study, and, because it was expected of him, shut the door behind him. What a strange night, what with the moon and the stars and all the other junk! Since it was all high above the treetops, the light seemed to dribble down. Lichtenberg had some books, but he wasn't reading any of them. The moon climbed higher and still higher, then it went down again. Lichtenberg watched it go. Because it had gotten warm, in the succession of the seasons, he had left the window open. He had pulled a chair up to the window, softly, softly. Then he was once more huddled in front of her door, breathing on it. He hoped the girl would stir, or perhaps call his name. But she didn't call it. Why would she have called it, anyway? He reached for his wastebook. "While he wanted to write," he wrote, "he remembered the house where he was born, and the voice of the steps when someone came up to him, the voices and the rhythm with which people would climb up to him." Or: "Will Tuesday the 10th really turn out to be the day of my death, as I dreamed yesterday it would? Perhaps so, but in what year?"

When he quietly stood up, not far from his girl—there was just a wall between them—and put his good ear to the door, he could hear something. There was some activity in her room. Lichtenberg told himself, she's up, the day is beginning. Because he didn't like to stand in the mornings, he sat down again. What was happening with the light? Bain-Marie had crawled out of her bed. You could hear her dinning in her little hole. Then she scratched at his door. When she asked why he hadn't been sleeping, he lied and said he had just got up. From now on, he thought, I shall have to tell more lies than ever, many more!

Unfortunately, Bain-Marie had taken a dislike to the Stechardess. She didn't mind showing it either. When the little girl tried to talk to her, she said: I don't talk to you! You create nothing but confusion around here! Now, she only carried the food as far as the door of Lichtenberg's room. There she left it in a corner, and Lichtenberg had to bring it to table himself. He said: I'll see what I can do! but there was always something he forgot: the bread or the little ham or the pickled cucumbers or the honey to drizzle in the tea. Bain-Marie chortled in her corner each time there was something missing. When he had finally got everything ready, he crossed his hands behind his back and trotted once round the table. Then he called out: Ready! and straightened his silk necktie. Any minute her door would open, and the little Stechardess would appear.

Between eleven and one he had no teaching. Then he would sit at his marking table, correcting his students' work. He was "nervous and in love, a combination that sometimes occurs," he wrote. Sometimes students came, they were unable to read his marks on their papers. Then Lichtenberg and the little Stechardess would hardly see anything of each other. Or he stood in his room, with the rabbit's foot in his hand. He used that to wipe the dust off his electrophore, but it kept coming back just the same. Once more, as he liked to say, he found himself "on the scent of electricity as it occurs in nature." Its existence in dogs had been proven. "Now," he wrote to Johann Heinrich Hurter, "I am looking on my cat Meow. She's not interested, and resists me. What other option do I have, then, but gentle force? I therefore *compel* her to my table, frot her fur, and . . ."

In the evening, the two of them often sat together. Because Bain-Marie came less and less, the Stechardess made an attempt to cook and clean. But she thought she wasn't welcome, and only hesitantly went up to his door. He, for his part, supposed she didn't want to see him "on account of my disability." Or at least not close to, and in daylight. They were both mistaken.

In this way, they lived at cross purposes with one another, monosyllabically—he—and timidly—she.

No sooner was it light in the morning than he reached for his books, and went into the big room. It was often half-full already. There were lots of underlinings in the books. He thought the students wouldn't notice there was a woman living with him. He thought they wouldn't notice anything.

6.

*T*HIS ALL HAPPENED IN July, which, like his love, seemed to go on for ever that year. Lichtenberg, with an erection, ran around, calling: It must be the heat! Whenever the Stechardess wasn't with him, he pictured her instead. Sometimes she went home as it got dark, sometimes she stayed in the Gotmarstrasse. They seemed to be making friends. They laughed a lot together, which, he thought, couldn't hurt. When they ate, each was now familiar with the other's likings, the movements of his hands, of his mouth. They knew what the other liked to eat, and what he wouldn't touch. The Stechardess was less afraid of him now. She moved nearer to him, and laughed more than she did previously. Often she left the door to her room open. Lichtenberg, in his fine new coat, brushed past her more nearly. Once, she went to him and declared she wanted to help him.

Help me, exclaimed Lichtenberg, looking around. He didn't know what the Stechardess could do to help him. He said: I'll have a think about it!

At such moments, they drew nearer to one another.

When they happened to touch now, she didn't straightaway shrink back. They called one another "Du." She no longer accounted it peculiar if he stood in front of the bookshelves, talking to himself. She listened to him, and she nodded. Then she left the room, and said: Carry on, don't mind me! When he threw a heap of books into the corner, and shouted: All useless! she stooped to pick them up again. She said: Maybe they will come in useful, I mean, later! And she carried them back to the bookcase. She seemed to be getting used to the sight of his skull, with wig and without. When it got too hot in the room, he pulled off his wig, and she said: Oh!

Yes, he said, that's what I look like, net, so to speak, without what art drapes over me. Here, he said, look all you want, put your hand on it if you like!

The little Stechardess shook her head. Not today, she said, maybe another time!

Tomorrow, perhaps?

Maybe!

Then she would look at his grey hair, and how thin it was already. Let her see that I've been alive for longer than she has! She knows I have anyway, he thought to himself. When the girl stood in front of him like that, he said: My wig! and slid it round the table.

But what are you doing with it, she asked, and he said: I'm polishing the table!

At that, she had to laugh, and he laughed along. Once, by the window, she wanted "to show him something," and she took off her bonnet. That was the first time he saw her beautiful dark-blond hair. And the pretty back of her head, which was where, as she said, she was to be found.

In there, he asked.

Where else?

Like all girls, she liked stroking her hair and playing with it. Usually she kept her bonnet on, but she didn't mind letting it be seen sometimes either.

Do you want to see it, she asked him.

If I may!

It's all God's own handiwork, she said. Her hair was fine, and reached down to her hips. He was surprised. Did you think it would be so long?

No, he said, and he walked around her.

Yes, that's how long it is, she said, and she told him the story of her hair, about how she washed it and brushed it and hung it in the sun to dry. That was what made it so soft and shiny. Then she wanted to tuck it back under the bonnet, but he said: No, leave it be! She blushed, and shrugged her shoulders and said: Well, that's how it is, anyhow!

Lichtenberg stood her in the blind corner away from the window, and walked around her. The Stechardess, not yet thirteen, let him look at her hair. Then she suddenly said: All right, that's enough! and she went in her room, and shut the door behind her. Lichtenberg thought: Now I've frightened her! Maybe I pushed her too far. Never mind, she'll come back! And he sat down and wrote something. "I have been making experiments with electricity. I saw that an electric shock produces masses of concentric circles in powdered resin. Of course, it's all sport, but it's fine, instructive sport, that I needn't be ashamed of!" Then he took off his wig, pulled off his breeches, and crept into his untenanted bed, from which he crept the following morning. It was always very . . .

Very what?

Early!

7.

*A*T FIVE HE CREPT INTO HIS morning gown and went out into the garden for the healthful morning air. It wasn't just good for his health, it also made him younger. He looked back at his house a lot. There was something he had left behind there. Then along came Bain-Marie, with a glass of well water, the biggest he had. He followed it with a cup of bouillon, which chased it down his throat. The Stechardess was in her room, he left her in peace. At half past seven came the first of his students, filling his room with their exhalations. Then he would hold a book in his hand, from which he read aloud to them. Those words they didn't understand he wrote up on the blackboard. He was always engrossed in something, had his head "buried in something or other." And so until about two o'clock. Then he had himself driven to the Pauliner Strasse, and with his head full of the Stechardess—as opposed to having her by his side—he ate a little snack. Then it was time again. New students arrived. These too with notebooks under their arm, for Lichtenberg to "dictate into." If he happened to be unprepared, he told them something from the history of mathematics that he had read somewhere or just made up on the spot. He wasn't that fussed about history, it was all right to make it up. Only mathematics was serious. To conclude, he told them something out of his own life. Then the hall was full. He carried on, until his eyes were watering. Thereupon, he had himself driven out to the edge of town, to see "if everything was still there, the houses and trees and so on and so forth." When he returned to his room, he brought a couple of new sentences with him. At six, after inhaling and exhaling deeply once or twice, he was sitting next to the Stechardess in the bower, inhaling her smell. They talked about the grass and the sky and about how quickly the day passed. He ate a green salad with her and a cold fruit soup, but without honey, because that was bad for his teeth.

Then they walked around the garden together. Sometimes he looked up at her and asked: Am I walking too quickly for you, or is it all right like this?

No no, she said, it's just exactly right!

They reached the place where they could be seen through the fence from the Gotmarstrasse, and he said: So far and no further! There were growing things all over, and he told her what they were. She asked what it was good for, and he said: If something is particularly beautiful, it has no use at all! When it had gotten dark, she would whisk him up a little soup, and he would read to her by candlelight. Sometimes they would tell each other things about themselves: what they liked to eat and drink, what way it had to be boiled or roasted to be to their liking, and what time of the year they preferred, the warm or the cold. If something was the same for both of them, she said: Just like me! and he said they fitted together, even though he might be a little smaller and older, but not much, not much!

Then he escorted her to her room like a fine lady (her, not him). Soon they were both abed, "but each in his own." Then everything blurred for her. On weekends, they sat in the bower. Or they might be standing under the sky, looking "at superfluous items, such as flowers." The Stechardess would always point them out, and Lichtenberg would sometimes circumambulate them. Winged by her smile and her presence—and her youth, of course!—which lifted him "three feet off the ground," he succeeded the following morning "in getting an uncommonly large and stout pig's bladder to rise." (Pigs' bladders, also amniotic sacs—*amnia*—sold to him by a midwife for four pfennigs a piece, were a staple of his scientific equipment.) When in his dressing gown he passed one such inflated sac, it would skip in the air, and follow him a while. The Stechardess would point at it and call: Look, how funny! It's following you! Sometimes the sac would skip over the ground, and sometimes it would float in the air, always with its tied end pointing to the ground.

And then?

When Lichtenberg came back exhausted from his seminar, she would tell him things. Often she would talk about her siblings. He would tell her how, many years ago, he had moved to Darmstadt, with his boy's hunchback. He remembered how they had all "gawped at his hunchback." When his mother saw her little boy wasn't going to grow any more, she said: Come here, you permanent shrimp! She put him in boots with thick soles, "you couldn't get them any higher"! And that was the limit of what she could do for him. He breathed more than the others did.

Often he would stand by the garden gate, telling her things. At school, he sat right at the front, so that the teachers could listen to his breathing. Then they would know that he was still all right. The school janitor's name was Hammer, and so he was known as "the Ax." He pulled Lichtenberg by the ears. Now just you listen to me, sonny, he said, and he told him to start growing. Did you understand what I said, he asked, and Lichtenberg said: I think so, sir! But he was always just saying that, in reality it didn't occur to him for a moment. He thought: I'll stay as I am! They called him "the baboon," and cried: Isn't he sweet? He was apt to snort through his nose, sometimes through his mouth. The noise he made was copied by his enemies . . .

What enemies, asked the Stechardess, and Lichtenberg said: Well, that's how it was! Because one day he knew he had some. They stood all around him, snorting at him. It was such fun. Then Lichtenberg burst into tears, and ran off with his hunchback.

What else, asked the Stechardess on another occasion. Lichtenberg scratched at his wig. In his head it was morning again, but a different morning. It was the time he was knitting. He would sit cross-legged in the corner, on the floor, so people didn't see him. It was either late autumn or winter, cold anyway. The animals and the people were cold. Some, who had been extant this past twelvemonth, were now no more. Little Lichtenberg looked for them for a while. Then he said: Well, that's the way the cookie crumbles! and he forgot them. His mother wedged a cushion under him and said: There! People were coming and going. Lichtenberg held something in his hands that rattled, cool pointy needles. If his father happened not to be preaching, he would be sitting facing him. I ought to look at this curious specimen a little more often, thought the Father, after all, he is my son!

And then?

Then, said Lichtenberg, he moved next to me, I could feel his warmth. Sometimes I fell asleep. Father took the needles away from me, in case I hurt myself. They were a present from him. So that I might be distracted from my body—which was a temporary prison that I would soon leave behind me. Then Father went away again, and little Lichtenberg pushed a needle under his linen shirt. You could scratch better that way. First he scratched his soft belly, then he scratched his tough hunchback. He got quite carried away with it, and wouldn't stop. When the blood came running and he had to stop, he cried: Oh, that was lovely!

And then, asked the Stechardess.

Then, said Lichtenberg, I carried on with my knitting, a scarf for my father. Sometimes in brown, more often in black. I rolled it up lovingly, and held it out to him. He accepted it, said: Another one! and put it with the others. Then I sat around, pondering what I ought to knit or say or think now.

He liked best to sit at the table by the window, or in the doorway. Both were near the exit. Sometimes someone would come in. Well, said Mother, won't you stand up when a visitor comes to look at you? So Lichtenberg stood up. He didn't want to be any bigger, or any straighter. And what do you do when a gentleman comes to see us, asked his mother. Am I to show him my hunchback, asked Lichtenberg. Yes, said his mother, then you show him your hunchback! The visitor was leaning in a corner, looking at his hunchback. When Lichtenberg was sitting down again, looking at his stitches, the visitor asked: Does he do anything else? Is he getting any bigger at last? and his mother replied: I don't think so! And she led the visitor round him a couple of times, so that he might view his industry and his hunchback from all sides. The visitor said: Thank you! and went home again.

In summer, Lichtenberg sat outside the house, letting the sun shine on him. He was waiting for a happy childhood, but it didn't seem to want to come. It's just a rumor, he thought, this happy childhood, like so much else! Then he took a mouthful of wine, that made it easier to speak. He had more ideas then, too, and that was never bad. Another time was on Sunday. He was sitting in the bower with the Stechardess. She had on a new dress. He was to tell her something new. Because she kept asking: And then?

What I told you, said Lichtenberg, is quite some time ago. At the time his mother was still alive. Even his father was still alive, and making his noises. Lichtenberg held his knitting needles in his hands. Often he was just knitting in his head. That would sometimes itch. Curious—it was easier to scratch with the left than the right. He lived in his head. He had settled in there, and wasn't going to come out. When he hadn't thought about his hunchback for a long time, he had a meeting. It was outside the town, on the way to Weende. As ever, he was walking along, following his nose, planning nothing bad. Then some man he didn't know would step out, asking to look at his hunchback. There might be two of them. Lichtenberg took off his little coat, to make it easier for them to see it. Slowly, with their hands behind their backs, they circled around it. When they had seen it, they nodded and said: OK, that's enough! Lichtenberg slipped his coat back on and called: You're welcome! Then he gritted his teeth and didn't turn to watch them. That was in his early years, or else in his head, which had no years. Everything there happened simultaneously or in a variable order, because knitting . . .

He had been taught to knit, even before reading and writing, by his tutor Palisander. When he rested his back against a wall once, his hunchback appeared. He hadn't known at the time that it would stay there. Well, well, he thought, and he rubbed it against the wall. When his hunchback refused to go away, he went to his room and cried. When his father stopped appearing on the grounds that he was dead, he shook his head and refused to believe it. Later, when he was forced to believe . . . The sun shone in his face again. Already, he was reading a lot. "The world," he read, "is an instrument which is often directed against mankind." Everything he read bypassed his head, and went straight into his books. Yes, he thought, the sun!

And then, asked the Stechardess.

Old Frau Piehler, who was to look after him on that day, took him by the hand. To distract him from the death of his father, she led him into the garden. There he trod on a few flowers. She dragged him around for a while. She was wearing a bonnet that had a grease spot on it. Lichtenberg fixed on it as he walked and stood. From now on, whenever he thought of death, he would think of a bonnet with a grease spot on it. (And vice versa: Whenever he saw such a bonnet . . .) Frau Piehler talked about his father, though as about something in the past. When little Lichtenberg asked: And when is he coming back? she said: Never! Then they were back at the garden gate. Lichtenberg ran into the house to see if his father might not have returned *after all*, but he wasn't there yet. Frau Piehler heated up a pan of milk for him, and then shut him up in his room. He sat or stood or lay around. After that, he must have fallen asleep.

And then he didn't go to the funeral. He was at home, by the window. No funeral for him, people said. He's too sensitive! He stood in the kitchen by the tub of sauerkraut, crying at the wall. His father, who had always been there, was now not to be there any more. Was it not monstrous and unfathomable?

At any rate, he wasn't allowed to go to the funeral then. He had to bury his father in his head. Father was nicely dressed, and was wearing his dog collar. Lichtenberg was talking and talking to him, but his father didn't reply. Father, cried the little Lichtenberg, say something! or: Father, why don't you speak! But he didn't speak. He lay in the middle of the room, and Mother was just crying and crying. The neighbors crossed themselves, and walked around him. Then they began to yawn, and one of them said: Well, that's enough of that! Then Father was bundled up, and quickly driven to the graveyard. A hole was dug for him, and he was laid in it. But the little Lichtenberg didn't actually witness all these things, he just imagined them for himself. But when he shut his eyes, Father and the hole in the ground kept coming back. Especially when it was dark, and he wanted at last to get off to sleep. It went on like that for weeks. One time the door opened, and his mother came in. She asked: What are you up to? and he said: I'm looking at the ceiling! Yes, said his mother, but what's going on *inside* you? and Lichtenberg said: I'm passing the time! He might be small and a queer fish, but already he harbored vast feelings inside him. Hence, the inevitable: his first love! It was at second sight. They were supposed to be days like all the rest, and now he would never forget them.

And then, asked the Stechardess.

8.

*I*N GÖTTINGEN—POP. 10,000—there were no secrets. One person yanked another around the corner, and the whispering began. Often enough, the subject was Dr. Lichtenberg and the beautiful child. They watched him go about, and they shook their heads. He was wearing a new coat, which had not yet been paid for. His collar no longer lay down upon his shoulders, but stuck up in the air. He had new thoughts as well. Ever since he'd met the girl, they were bubbling out of him. Then he called to her, pointed to his brow, and said: I've got so much stuff coming out of here, look! and when she asked: So much of what? he said: That stuff I paste together! Most of his thoughts were about her, the rest were of a scientific or speculative nature. They concerned an adjustable table that a Mr. Nairne had built for him in London, and which, with the appropriate machinery, was to cost one hundred and eight talers.

His preferred working place was not the university, but home in the Gotmarstrasse, at his three tables. He had pulled off his little coat and hung it on the wall. When he passed it, he said: Brand new! and tugged at it. There was always heaps of stuff lying on his tables. He pushed it this way and that, and said: Oh, you too! I'd forgotten about you! Then he heard her next door again. He took up his quill, his "provisional instrument for immortality," and wrote something down with it. "A book," he wrote, "is like a mirror. When a monkey looks into it . . ." Oh no, he'd had that one already! He crossed it all out again. He had taken off his waistcoat, and rolled up his sleeves. The Stechardess was next door, he could hear her.

When he had thought himself into a problem—he had just proposed a theory of Lichtenbergian figures—the child seemed to be able to sense it. At any rate, he heard her sigh. When he had solved—or thought he had solved—a problem, he shouted to her: I've got it! or: It's in the bag! and she shouted: Because I was crossing my fingers for you! and she started to sing. That gave him courage.

When a problem was too big for his head, he worked with equipment: his areometer from Darmstadt, the hydrostatic scales, his Magdeburg hemisphere to prove air pressure, and so on and so forth. They all stood in his biggest room, in the corner "where there first had to be thinking and then proving." Once, he asked her: Do you see my thoughts? and she replied: Am I meant to see them?

On occasions, old Bain-Marie still came. When she stood in front of him, he noticed she was taking away his time. Then he called: Hurry, hurry! and shooed her out the door. She said: It's all right, I'm on my way! and she disappeared. When the Stechardess was with him, he fetched a chair for her and said: Please sit down! But she shook her head and said: I'd sooner stand! Lots of things accumulated in his working corner. He pointed at them with his finger and said: Signs of life!

Sometimes he took her by the hand to lead her round the room. He showed her his books and folders and told her about what was in them. This is where I put the world under the magnifying glass. And under the minimizing glass too, for that matter, he said. He wanted to make a note of the expression, which had "leapt upon him in the course of speech," but then he let it go. He pushed bits of equipment this way and that, and explained them to her. The dust that fell from planing the resin field of an electrophore flew off at the slightest commotion. On one occasion, it had failed to settle equally over everything. Rather, to his pleasure—"no, to my good fortune, my good fortune!"—little stars had formed that, to begin with, had been dim and hard to recognize. When he sprinkled on the dust more thickly, the stars became quite distinct, and resembled "magnificent works of art." He had brought off innumerable little stars, whole Milky Ways and solar systems, pretty little capillaries that resembled those the ice makes on window panes, clouds of variable form and hue. Now Lichtenberg and the pretty child were hunkered down before them, gaping in wonder. It was a charmed world, and neither of them knew what it meant. The Stechardess saw only its beauty, but Lichtenberg, "the objective scientist," wanted to hypothesize from it, and use the beauty to a certain end he didn't yet know, and to draw conclusions from it.

Yes, but what conclusions, asked the Stechardess, and what for?

For hours, which simply flew by as Time does when one isn't careful, they hunkered there and "observed the beauty." The Stechardess sat hard by him. They sat there for a long time.

What were you doing just now, she asked suddenly.

I was studying the wonders of nature.

For all that time?

Yes, for all that time!

When they ran their fingers over them, the stars proved indestructible. They were for all time. When he took a hen's feather or a rabbit's foot, and carefully attempted to wipe away the dust, similar figures were formed, even more beautiful than the ones before. Lichtenberg, "the ugly devotee of beauty," was enraptured, and cried out: A miracle! Quick! Look!

The Stechardess always came right away. She had her bonnet on. They stood side by side, inspecting the miracle together.

As the "marks of celestial beauty" had made their appearance shortly after the Stechardess—in a light skirt and bonnet—Lichtenberg believed the two things, the girl and the miracle dust, were connected. One beauty must have brought the other in its train. That caused him to ponder. He pulled the street curtain to the side, so that he could see something without being seen himself, the little voyeur. The Stechardess was standing behind him, she couldn't be seen from the street. Because it would make people talk about her even more, she didn't leave the house now. As he wasn't allowed to love her, he was getting a rash in his face. It looked awful, especially in daylight, all over his cheeks and forehead. As always when something oppressed him, he had to talk about it.

The human body, which to all of us is a miracle and a riddle and possibly—let's not be afraid to say so—a divine creation, often goes off the rails, he said. Then we say that it's unwell. Do you understand what I'm trying to tell you, he asked, holding a handkerchief in front of his face.

Yes, she said, you're unwell!

You shouldn't look at me then, he said. It looks awful, doesn't it?

The child laughed. If you're referring to the thing on your forehead, she said, that doesn't bother me!

Really, he asked.

In Göttingen, where people talked about everything under the sun, they talked about him a lot too. The town had been part of the Hanseatic League, but in the Thirty Years' War it had come down in the world. Then it had belonged to the English crown. For a time there was a lot of English spoken there. When people ran out of things to say to each other, they liked to "badmouth one another." They said that Professor Schlichtegroll had spent last night in the gutter again, and had had to be "fished out." The following day, they talked about Professor Kästner. They said he had a daughter by a hatmaker who was herself young enough to be his daughter. The woman was pointed out when she walked through Göttingen with Kästner's daughter. And women anyway! The wife of Pastor Hase was supposed to be a real goer. Herr Hase knew it, but what could he do? There were more children born out of wedlock than in. One person in five suffered from an unmentionable disease. Sometimes Lichtenberg mentioned "that part of oneself that one didn't mention either," calling it "his little *bel ami*." People still hadn't got used to Lichtenberg and his "withered aspect." He couldn't walk across the road without people saying something droll about him, like: Small, but quite a handful! or: Do you see something creeping towards us!

Yes, replied someone, if it ever gets that far!

He spends too much time squatting at his desk!

Because he's ink-continent!

It was the first time in a long time that Lichtenberg was walking in such close proximity to people. They smelled his sweat. Their eyes and their ears boggled, not one of them shrank away from him. Because the Stechardess was now eating and sleeping at his house—not with him, mind!—they had abrogated their greeting. He had to go on greeting them, though. Then he was past them, and they spun round to look at him from behind. He didn't really notice at all, he was lost in thought. Often it would be thinking about some favorite notion of his, for instance: Is the cause of all movement in the world an idea of God's? Lichtenberg nodded and smiled subtly and said: It's possible! And resolved that he would go and sit in the third of his rooms today and look into the matter.

At first blush, everything in the lecture hall was the same as usual. When the students saw his rash, they pointed at it and said: There it is! or: It's flourishing! There was a smell in the library of book dust and erudition. Yes, it's my element, cried Lichtenberg, and would have liked to run off. With his books under his arm, he climbed the steps. Before he knew it, they were all around him: Kästner, Gatterer, Schlichtegroll. They were all agitated, they had been talking about him. Today they weren't going to be pushed aside, not by any little Court Councillor!

Gentlemen, he cried, excuse me, excuse me, excuse me! and he thought: How can I get rid of them? He wanted to go on!

Kästner, Gatterer and Schlichtegroll made for him. They hemmed him in. Hey, Lichtenberg, they cried and they stood around him. There was no escape.

A word with you, please, said Dr. Gatterer. He raised his hand.

We hardly see you any more, said Kästner. Are you engrossed in some scientific investigation?

Have you, asked Dr. Gatterer, lost your heart to some scientific task? and they all laughed. Lichtenberg laughed with them.

What sort of research is it, asked Kästner, is it straightforward or ticklish? Will it be extended, or speedily concluded? Are her eyes blue or brown?

What, exclaimed Lichtenberg, and they all laughed again. Dr. Schlichtegroll clapped his hands in merriment.

Yes, said Dr. Kästner, the times have changed! Once, I remember one only had to take a walk through the town and one was certain to encounter your amusing little personage. And now one can tramp through our beautiful Göttingen for hours on end, without sighting you. It's as though you weren't with us any more! Is it true that you spend all your time at home, twiddling your thumbs?

Yes, said Lichtenberg, and now I must leave you!

Is it true that you always have someone sitting near you, asked Dr. Schlichtegroll, often very near you?

Perhaps you're expected at home now, asked Dr. Gatterer. So do tell, he cried, but already Lichtenberg had barged his way past the three of them—from below, from below!—and was running upstairs. Professor Kästner and Schlichtegroll and Gatterer all laughed after him.

People like that should have their buttons marked with zeroes, said Dr. Schlichtegroll.

No one can have been driven demented by love in such short order as he, said Gatterer, and they all went home. There, their books were waiting for them, for each his own.

At Lichtenberg's everything was as he had left it. He crept around the Stechardess, the dwarf around the girl. The nearer, the better! He loved her scent. It wasn't just the lavender, it was her skin. They carried on long conversations, with lots of nodding on either side. Then he cried: I must away to work! and ran out the door.

Then Lichtenberg couldn't see the girl any more, but at least he could still hear her. She spent a lot of time next door to him. When he lugged his head in front of the mirror, he saw this and that. For instance, he was losing his hair, by fistfuls now. My God, he exclaimed, that as well! He really needed his wig now. Because "in the march of the seasons" it was now summer, he took his wig off and laid it across his knee. Or he put it on the table, and slid it around this way and that. He really did look ugly now! He pictured the Stechardess, standing behind the window. Will I have enough time left for her, he wondered. When he ran his hand across his head, it was full of hair. So he stopped running it. Also, the dignity of his features depended on there being hair. If he pricked up his ears, he could hear the Stechardess next door. He pulled a chair over to the window, and looked out. There wasn't much to see. Clement weather that the Almighty had hung over Göttingen, and which . . . Fine, clement weather! The trees were of a summery green, if not worse. His chair was more elevated than the others, and so he liked sitting on it. When he was up on it . . . He thought about Gatterer, Schlichtegroll and the rest of them. There was plenty to say about them. He took his quill and a sheet of paper, and he wrote:

A list of terms, etc., for my friends:

Old trouser splutterer	Monkey face
Dirt on your beard (Arabic)	Lousy jack
Bear skinner	Fleabag
Barsteward	Gallowsbird
Shameshanks	Sow-waddle
Fool	Popinjay
Yellowbill	Snotspoon
Blackguard	Snortcock
Jackanapes	Poltroon
Woodenhead	Louse farmer
Toerag	Shitty shirt
Lowlife	Baccy beard

And for women, he thought, and wrote:

Hussy	Trull
Harlot	Carrion
Streetwalker	

Yes, he thought, snipe! There were, he thought, hundreds, nay, thousands more, but I'll draw a line here for want of time, space, paper, enthusiasm. I'll carry on tomorrow, if I remember.

9.

HEN CAME AUGUST, AND "the warmth they had yearned for all winter simply hung around everywhere." Just too much, too much, too much! Lichtenberg had his wig on, it was making him sweat. He had his spectacles perched on his nose, and was standing around in his flat. His glasses were dreadfully scratched, it was "from wanting to see too much." It wasn't actually Lichtenberg's flat at all, strictly speaking he didn't have one. Nor would he ever, he was just allowed "to walk up and down and sleep in it." His books were equally distributed all over the walls. Often one of them would trip him up, and he would shout: Devil take them! Or he cried: Book-fiends, you'll be the death of me yet!

Very well, not his property then! So whose?

His-publisher-Johann-Christian-Dieterich's-(1722–1800) who-permitted-little-Lichtenberg-to-live-in-his-house-for-free-out-of-the-goodness-of-his-heart. All Lichtenberg had to do in return was write something for him from time to time. So he sat down by the window, where he did his best writing. Like most of those who "dribble ink over paper for a living," he never became a householder. He had to be grateful that he was allowed to stay under the Dieterichs' roof. When an acquaintance passed, he drew his head in, so as not to be obliged to offer a greeting. He was wearing his professor's shirt. He had it buttoned up to the top to keep the Göttingen wind from getting in anywhere. Round his neck he had wound his best silk cloth, for her, for her, for her! There was the little bulge in front, and the big one at the back. He smiled and thought of, well, who do you think? What things looked like inside—"in the little cardiac chamber"—no one knew with him. That, he thought, is how my youth went, and now, if he wasn't careful, the rest would follow! The street behind his house was covered with dung in summer, from the passing livestock. When the sun shone on it . . .

No, not that please!

And when it rained, it was a quagmire. Then Lichtenberg made a detour past it, or else he stayed at home. Yes, such was his life! A shame he never discovered or invented anything of true substance in any of the sciences, and that he would one day die just like everyone else, obscure and quickly forgotten. He went into the big room. He was wearing shoes with purple buckles, which he struggled to reach. Even though I'm so close to the ground, he thought, looking down. Then he went in to the Stechardess.

I'm back, he said.

Ever since the Stechardess had moved into his flat—"stepped into his life"—Lichtenberg had dreamed a lot more. He only had to close his eyes, and there was the next dream already. He preferred dreaming of her. Or else he dreamed of an aerostatic machine, an enormous thing with which he wanted to flee the world. He wanted to get it up into the air, ideally in his garden. The children were standing by the fence, the neighbors were all waving. Lichtenberg had pulled his wig down into his forehead, and was waving as well. Then the balloon started to rise. "Attached to the bottom of it was a little basket, in which in my dream I was sitting. Next to me sat a sheep, a cock and a duck, which in the event of some mishap to me, were to report on our journey. The flying machine was painted blue and had golden festoons. And so we climbed and climbed into the air." The whole time, the Stechardess was standing by the kitchen window. She had thrown it wide open, and was gazing up at Lichtenberg. It was one of his failed experiments, nothing came of it. Comparisons with other researchers in France, in England, in Sicily, were humiliating. Whatever Lichtenberg had wanted to invent, these other characters had already done it. "If only we had more wealthy patrons of the sciences here in Göttingen, to put their money at our disposal," he wrote to Volta. The inventions of the French and the English were only possible because they had backing. But no one in Göttingen wanted to write a subscription so that the little Lichtenberg could finally discover something too. No one cared about science here, they were indifferent to it! There were nothing but obstacles here. Lichtenberg had to pay for everything he needed out of his own pocket. To fill his balloon with hot air, he needed to have a large room. Such as his lecture room, but that was only free in the semester vacations. When the balloon had finally been inflated, it couldn't fit through the door or the window. So Lichtenberg was left sitting with his balloon in the lecture room. He had crossed his legs, and was writing a letter. To one Dr. Schernhagen he complained about the "miserable world of Göttingen" that consisted of "nothing but pride, wage increases and book talk . . . But for a little thing of flesh and blood, I should be extremely lonely here, and could offer no objection to being placed under the ground eftsoons!"

The Stechardess had her bonnet on, and was sitting beside him. She looked at him sadly. What if they put you on the street, she asked.

I don't even think of that, he replied, I've got myself out of that habit!

She made efforts to give him encouragement. She sat in front of his apparatus and gazed at it lovingly. Sometimes she even petted it a bit. In the lecture room he told his children about "his ascent to the stars." When he was back from lecturing, she went to the stove. He had got through a day "that had produced nothing." He had "had to speak very loudly," once again they hadn't paid attention. And now the little fellow was exhausted. Later, following the failed tilt at science, their conversations became personal, even intimate. They took place, if the day was fine, on the green garden seat.

Wait a moment, she said, and got him a cushion.

Get yourself one too, he said, but she replied: I'm young, I don't have to sit soft!

The sun shone in their faces. He didn't appreciate so much sun, once he'd arrived at the conclusion that it didn't help him grow. Go away, sun, he always cried, and waved it away with his necktie. He was in his green coat, with no wig, "I don't care a pin for it!" He was holding it in his hand, and was plucking at it industriously. They spoke of the siblings they had had, he and she. Most of them were already dead.

Who all, asked the Stechardess, I mean who of yours?

Oh Lord, said Lichtenberg, with sigh. Then he began to list his dead: his father and mother and two sisters and two brothers and uncles and nephews and nieces he had either barely known or else long forgotten, or both. Sometimes they had paid visits to look at his hunchback. Now they wouldn't come any more. They had "got stuck on their procession through the world."

And then?

Well, said Lichtenberg, and then indeed.

He spoke about other people too, as they happened "to move through his head, one after the other." That was "a little funeral procession, running this way and that." The Stechardess looked at her knees, and stroked them. It was different with her. She didn't know that many people, her world was smaller. She just nodded and didn't speak. Then Lichtenberg took a deep breath and, quite unprompted, turned the conversation to women.

To what?

To women!

Of whom, he freely admitted, he didn't know much, he found them strange, even uncanny. What went on in their heads he had no idea at all, he "went the long way round it." The earliest, he said, he had . . . The old story. The earliest he had known at all had been the "cleaning women" the University sent his way. Always early in the morning, sometimes the sun wasn't even up. Armed with their mops and their buckets they had charged past "his scientific essays" and invaded his lecture room, "breaking something essential" on their way. Incredible creatures, he said, then blushed.

Why incredible, asked the Stechardess, and Lichtenberg said: They materialized with songs on their lips!

But why . . .?

Because of my . . . infirmity! You see, I've got this thing here, he said, pointing to his hunchback.

You would hardly know it's there, she said.

Oh yes, he said, when you look carefully! Had she not noticed it before, he asked, and she said: Not really! and when he wanted to talk about it some more, she said: It doesn't bother me! and he said: My little hunchbacklet! and they both laughed. So let's talk about something else then! he said, and started to talk about love.

About what?

Yes!

Lichtenberg looked at his nails and told her about his first . . . The Stechardess really didn't want to hear. She had stepped out of the sunshine, shook her little head, and looked at him earnestly. Sometimes she asked him something. All these women . . .

Not so many!

All right, she said, then: These few women, had he forgotten them again, and he said: Ah, memory! And he knocked on his head and said: They're in there! and: It's as with everything else. Sometimes they retire, and you think: Forgotten, forgotten! But then they're back, as shiny as new.

Who are?

Past ladies!

And why are they shiny? Tell me: Why are they shiny? Did he, she asked, sometimes speak of them?

I don't see them any more, so how can I describe them? Admittedly, if I had to . . .

You could!

I expect so, said Lichtenberg. One used to have her hands on her hips when I was with her. That was her style.

What about the others?

They swung them to and fro. Occasionally, they had taken a few steps at his side, as women to be touched.

And who were they?

One was old Samson's daughter, an old Platonic love, then there was the painters' model Justine, who, up to the point of her marriage, occasionally . . . Well, he said, gave or lent herself, if you like.

I see!

Then there was my passion for the "Comet," of whom no one knew anything for a long time. You, he said, are the first to hear about it. Behind the name, everyone had suspected the tailor's daughter Marie Sachs, and rightly. Finally there was his affair with a cook, also by the name of Marie. Tongues had also wagged about a beggar girl, said Lichtenberg, but at that the Stechardess suddenly motioned and said: I don't want to hear any more!

Doesn't it interest you?

Not very much, said the Stechardess. She yawned. Then she stepped out of the sun, and went to her room. She left her door open, though.

10.

*S*INCE LICHTENBERG AS A child was apt to go over on his stick legs, he was careful later always to wear stout boots. But the reason he never broke anything was because he never *wanted* to break anything. (Much later, he was forever breaking things, and had to be carried a lot.) Often he brought "sweets for his sweet," or a picture book, once it was a couple of chopsticks from Manchuria and once a pomegranate which the discoverer Reimarus (1729–1814) had brought back from Italy. The pomegranate sat on her windowsill a long time, they sniffed at it together.

Well, he asked, how does it smell? and she beamed and said: Good!

All the things he had merely thought previously, and that had preoccupied him as a bachelor, he now told her: that the weather had used to be warmer, and that his hunchback had shot out of him one black day. But let's talk about something else! he said. Then he went back to talking about his school, the *dungeon*, that he was able to leave six times a week for home. And that was when it had happened.

What had happened, asked the Stechardess.

His eye had lit for the thousandth time on the top boy in his class in Darmstadt, the tailor's son, W. Schmidt, and suddenly everything had changed.

Like what?

It was, said Lichtenberg, the day on which . . . They had given him a trim. His hands were . . . Well, what do you think? Ink-stained, he cried, ink-stained! After that, there was no getting round the fact that he had a hunchback.

He had seen W. Schmidt every day for years on end, but on that day he saw him differently.

Ooh, said Lichtenberg, and he clutched at his heart. Quickly he looked away from Schmidt. First he looked up to the heavens, then he looked down at the ground. Love had suddenly appeared, and from then on Lichtenberg had to scale the school walls to watch W. Schmidt walk away, and that was just one example. Schmidt went around in shorts and had long bare legs. His knees were dark and scabby. My God, thought Lichtenberg, and he wanted to stroke those legs, only he didn't dare. Often Schmidt walked along at his side, and he caught the smell of his skin. Schmidt went as far as the crossroads, and then he vanished. After he was gone, Lichtenberg could still see him "in his heart." He continued to hang around there. In the evening, Lichtenberg went outside with him, at night he saw him in his sleep. He transformed his nights. If he had hitherto seen his dead father in his dreams, he now saw his live friend. Sometimes, generally on warm days, they were together. They trotted along the lanes, and Lichtenberg touched him. Sometimes he touched him on the hand, sometimes on the arm. Because he had the feeling he ought to say something, he said: Ooh, you! W. Schmidt pulled his hand away, and said: Why are you barging into me? I'm not barging into you, replied Lichtenberg, I just got too near. Then stop it, said Schmidt, stop getting too near!

And then, asked the Stechardess.

Because Lichtenberg wanted to appear taller than he was, he already went around in high boots. His father hadn't taken his with him. They were on the boot rack, waiting for the little fellow to grow into them. It would take a while yet. When he was lying on his hunchback in bed with his eyes shut, he saw the tailor's son, and he sometimes felt a sensation. It was between his legs, and he thought: That must be your heart! He had occasionally been aware of it before, but never so strongly. And like that he fell asleep. Lichtenberg, his hunchback to the wall, started to dream.

And what happened then?

Along with thinking of love, came "the other thing," Lichtenberg said. It was another fine day. They were sitting facing one another, breathing over each other. The first thought of it came one winter, along with the snow that fell out of the sky, after class. Lichtenberg sat in the empty school, staring out of the window. He didn't want to be at home, he was too much alone there. He had climbed on top of his desk. He liked to climb up on chairs and tables and desks, it made him bigger. At any rate, no one could tell how big—or small—he was. So he was standing on the desk, reading something on the board, something to do with the declension of the word *domus*. Then, without his having thought any evil, *the other* was suddenly there. Lichtenberg leapt off the desk, that's how strong it was. But even the word "strong" is inadequate. It was the most overwhelming thought he had ever had, lying, sitting, or standing. With his hunchback to the wall, he felt his heart, just as then, when he had first *properly* seen W. Schmidt. He went to the desk, in which he had carved his name. That would outlast him! Lichtenberg took a deep breath and did what he would in the future always do with his thoughts: He wrote it down! The thought he wrote down now was simple enough. It was—what else could it have been?—a brief defense of suicide. "My friends," he wrote, "I can distinctly imagine my own death! It will be thus," he wrote and wrote and wrote.

And, asked the Stechardess.

Since suicide was no small matter, Lichtenberg had a lot to write. He sat all alone in the schoolroom, that was where he felt happiest. Outside, the wind was blowing across the snow, almost a warm wind. Lichtenberg thought ahead to the time he would no longer be there. "Friends," he wrote, "I'm standing in front of the curtain! I pull it back to see what's behind it, if there is anything behind it. I'm too tired to march on, I fall behind. Here, Nature, take back the material from which you've made me! Knead it into the mass of dead creation over which you rule, make a shrub or cloud out of it! Away with the curtain," wrote little Lichtenberg at his chair. He had seated himself on three fat cushions, and wrote and wrote and wrote. At last, the sun—the howmanieth?—had gone down, the candle burnt down, he folded up his piece of paper and blew out the stump.

How old were you then?

Well, said Lichtenberg, who could say! At any rate he had carried the piece of paper about with him ever since. When his mother found it, and asked what was on it, he said: A poem! After a few weeks, he took it out again, smoothed it down, and took it to Rector Wenck. He scratched on the Rector's door. He had to scratch way down low, he couldn't reach any higher. The Rector cried: Who's that scratching? and Lichtenberg replied: The little fellow! The Rector was wearing a woollen cap, and said: Come in, if you happen to be outside! But wipe your feet first! and when Lichtenberg had wiped them, he went in. He pressed the page about death into the Rector's hand, and said: I've got something for you! The Rector put on his nickel spectacles and read over the scrap of paper. He shook his head. He even wagged his finger at him, and started to chase away the idea in Lichtenberg's head, for all time. Finally, he tugged at Lichtenberg's ears, to make sure the idea never came back. Got it, he asked. Got it, replied Lichtenberg. Only for the time being, or for ever and ever, asked the Rector, and Lichtenberg replied: For ever and ever!

And then?

The thought did return, not often, but it did, and when Lichtenberg went on growing—not a lot, but he did!—the thought grew with him. Lichtenberg sat in his corner, gazing up at the ceiling. Then he went into a different corner, and gazed up again. Because the summer had come, there were flies around. Lichtenberg had made himself a fly swatter out of a floor rag. He hit, and he hit hard. Because his mother had now gone on as well, he was even more alone. (He said *allalone*.) His brothers and sisters were out in the world, only he was still at home. He noticed this and that about himself, and about others. What he noticed about himself were lots of new thoughts, and his fingernails. Sometimes he chewed them. Often he thought of *the thought* he had promised to forget, but wasn't able to forget. If he didn't want to think of *that*, he thought about his father. Something very curious must have happened to him by now in his little hole in the ground. Lichtenberg pulled on his boots, and set off to visit him. The hours were warm and bright, and he took off his jacket. Sometimes he hung it on his hunchback. Then he said: And now for something different! and he swung at the flies. And then, at last, the graveyard! He walked round it a couple of times, keeping his distance. His mother had been younger than his father, but now she had gone to join him. How awful it all was! Lichtenberg would have liked to say something about it, but he couldn't think of what to say. The time I spent with them was over so quickly, how could it be, he thought. That day passed quickly as well. The sun, which had been up at the zenith, was now down at the bottom of the sky. He pulled on his coat again. He left his father and mother to each other, and trotted home.

He thought of a new speech about suicide, this time in Latin. In '57 he delivered it in front of his school. They all stood around him, and hoped he would slip up. Rector Wenck and his master Palisander were there too. They had their eyes closed, but their ears were open. Lichtenberg had gone over to the wall, where he could hear himself speak properly. He needed his head for that. If you drifted down from there, you encountered the hunchback and then the belly. His speech came out right at the top, next to the open window. All that happened in that year. His parents didn't have to die any more, they were already dead. Sometimes his body wanted to divide itself. Lichtenberg had gone over to the stove, so he could listen to it crackling. Snow was falling outside again, but that was in a different year. First it covered the trees and the roofs, and then it covered the people. The world was transformed! Lichtenberg, with the thing on his back, sat quietly in his corner. He was sitting next to himself too, and watching himself sitting. Quite right, there were two of him! These two, Lichtenberg and himself, had never been so much at one. He was knitting again. People talked at him from all sides. He very rarely said anything back. He looked down the street. If someone passed, he quickly shut his eyes so as not to be seen. His father and mother were lying in their double hole, each on his side. He thought about them a lot. He sat over his books and papers, he really crept into them. He spent a lot of time scribbling now, though it never amounted to very much. Patience! he said to himself. Then he cupped his knee in his hand. Yes, it was his knee! With his other hand, he cupped the other knee. Yes, that was the second!

And then?

The first poem he wrote was at this time as well. It was the description of a kitchen garden, but it was done in hexameters! Afterwards he came down with fever, and was put to bed. He always had plenty of thoughts, he didn't know where they came from. All he had to do was shut his eyes, and there was the next one already. There were two kinds, scientific and other. There was an audience for the scientific ones, the others he wrote for himself. Although he was often alone in his room, he kept his notebook locked in his desk drawer. Then he pulled it out. "I get through a lot of ink," he wrote. "I need to be careful not to spill it over my trousers, that have seen plenty of spillage already in the course of my life!" Because the Stechardess was nearby, he was happy. "Careful!" he wrote, "things are looking up for me!" Then he crossed something out, and wrote: "Careful! Things *might* be looking up for me!" Yes, that was more like it! He had his wig on, and was thinking about happiness and unhappiness. When he had done that, he went over to the window and thought about something else: this time it was health and illness, and how they were related. The Stechardess wore her pink bonnet, and his happiness was bound up with her. No, she was his happiness! Round her neck, she wore a kerchief, which he sometimes helped her tie. She had to bend down for him, otherwise he couldn't have got up there. Come down here, he said, and she replied: I don't mind if I do! Then they both smiled. Or she looked over his shoulder while he philosophized. "To feel again," he wrote, "a happiness to which we have become inured, we need only to imagine that we had lost it, and only found it again at that moment . . ."

What do you mean by that, asked the Stechardess.

I'm picking up a previous thought.

What was it about?

Happiness, said Lichtenberg, what else?

Then he gave her his notebook so that she could see for herself what he had written about happiness. She said: I'm sure it's all well and good, but I can't read!

Ah, of course, said Lichtenberg, I'd forgotten! Would you like me to teach you?

Yes!

Very well, he said, we'll start tomorrow!

11.

WHAT WAS GOING through Lichtenberg's head at the time—"through my various heads"—was generally of a scientific nature. He held his notebook aloft and preserved his thoughts "for the sake of posterity, which won't want to read them." Often they were about the pros and cons of living. Lichtenberg was generally pro, though he felt guilty because he didn't see much point in it. "What have I done with the past three months," he wrote, and appended a large question mark. "Eaten, drunk, electrified, laughed over a young kitten and played with a little girl," he wrote. "Where have the five thousand years of the world gone, in which *I* lived?" Then he said: Stick to the point! and he looked down the Gotmarstrasse. He reflected, but this time not about the whole kit and caboodle. He thought of details, particulars, individuals. He thought of his benefactor Dieterich, who saved him from starving. As it got dark, they often strolled around the neighborhood together. They passed lots of houses.

What is it, asked Lichtenberg, that makes a town a town?

I give up, said Dieterich, and Lichtenberg said: Light and darkness!

I see, said Dieterich.

They were arm in arm, like a couple. The street was awash with mud. In case one of them stumbled, the other would keep him standing. Since Lichtenberg, with his short legs, couldn't keep up, he called out: Not so fast!

Forgive me, my dear friend, said Herr Dieterich, I was thinking of something else!

The structure, said Lichtenberg, that carries everything aloft: body, head, thoughts . . .

Don't worry, said Herr Dieterich. I won't run away from you!

Lichtenberg had a place at Herr Dietrich's table, and on the sofa among his children who went by Wilhelm, Liese, August, and so on and so forth. Sometimes he mixed them up. Then the child would cry: I'm not August!

I know you're not, said Lichtenberg, perfectly calmly, I misspoke!

There were always two children perched on his knees. The others huddled around him and stroked his hunchback. Does that hurt, they asked. Often they all asked at the same time.

Not at all, replied Lichtenberg blithely. Not with your little children's hands! They feel quite nice!

Nevertheless, that's not something you do to such a dear guest, said Frau Dieterich, wagging her finger. Then she cried out: Stop your messing about! Leave the Herr Doktor alone! Then she clapped her hands. That was the signal for coffee to be brought.

Because he had now met the Stechardess, Lichtenberg got impatient at the Dieterichs'. By now she would be sitting waiting for him, either at her own table or his. Or so I hope anyway, that she is waiting and not run off somewhere, he thought.

The Dieterichs of course knew everything, but they pretended they didn't know. Lichtenberg tugged at his wig a while, and then he went on. He claimed he needed to write something down, "something important," he said. In point of fact, he was forever writing. "Anywhere he goes, he's extending his horizons and his love," he wrote. "Yesterday, the little girlie twinkled at him. God knows where it's all going to end!"

As far as his thoughts were concerned, Lichtenberg was most often alone with them. "The man moves in a small, but elite society," he wrote. "He is on first name terms with everyone who has a Europe-wide reputation." He was in contact with Bernoulli, Delalande, Maskelyne, Messier, Cassini, with Mallet in Geneva and Rumowski in St. Petersburg. They all knew his handwriting, and not a few knew his hunchback as well. They wrote him clever letters asking after his welfare. He carried their letters with him a long time. Asked or unasked, he would sometimes pull them out of his pocket, and show them to people on the street or at home. He always replied to them. When he set foot in his study in the evening, there were always fresh letters waiting for him. When there was nothing to reply to, he had his wastebook. "Here the particulars of the world are governed by him," he wrote. "As soon as he's familiar with something, he sees that there is a lot of redundancy about it, and he recognizes that he should express it more pithily. Finally, he is so pithy that he cuts half of it and doesn't understand what he was trying to say!"

What were the notes in aid of? Something very peculiar: language! "For some time now, I've been trying to find its secret," he wrote.

Its secret, asked the Stechardess, looking at him in alarm.

Yes, he said, quite so!

He had become aware of it on his walks from room to room, and round about his thoughts. Now he imagined that there was a secret somewhere. Very well, but what is it? he asked himself. Along came the difficulties. He told himself that a word not only expressed the essence of a thing, but also its connections and its relationship to other words, and even its history. "And in addition of course," he wrote, "the undertones and overtones that come with the spoken word. If that could be captured in writing, it would be a way to extend language infinitely, without adding to the number of words," he wrote, "but whether... Time is no friend of ours," he wrote, and he wanted to capture some other important topic, but then he remembered the Stechardess, and forgot it. He sat there, feeling exhausted from his visit to the Dieterichs, going up and down stairs, all the conversations. Also, "autumn was hanging around outside," and people were doing a lot of talking. A country-swap had been planned, right outside the front door. Karl Theodor was to hand in Bavaria, and be given the Austrian Lowlands in return. In the end, nothing came of it. German was now introduced as the official language in Hungary, and in the Bay of Tchesme the Turkish fleet with twenty-three vessels was sunk by the Russian fleet. Oh dear oh dear!

The Stechardess was wearing her bonnet and sitting next door. Lichtenberg had retreated to his *thinking room*, but not far enough. Instead of Göttingen or London, he was thinking of other places, where he wasn't known, "places to be alone with her in." He lay on the sofa, the Stechardess thought he was asleep. He wanted to get her, but then he commanded himself: No, stay like this awhile longer! He returned to the span of his life, most of which was now up. He remembered "faces from bygone times." They came quite unsolicited, and he didn't know what to do with them, where to put them. Each of them moved with his characteristic movements, he recognized every one. They walked up his stairs: good old Hach with his horsehair, and Lichtenberg's old, now dead, headmaster who had always got at him because of the pretzel he kept under his coat. That's true, he thought, you're not allowed to eat in school, you have to leave it outside! He smiled once more, now the Stechardess would knock on his door any minute. He would call: Who is it now? and she would reply: It's me, and you know it is! Oh, he thought, she doesn't even knock! She scratches with her fingertips, like a sleepy beast. Well, I can hear her just the same!

Lichtenberg wasn't ready to think about her again just yet, he wanted to save that for later. He went back into his head, and ran into this and that. For instance, into the apple-spotted walls of his schoolroom, where he had always seen the hurly-burly of battle as it got dark. He thought of the scratched slate board, where the names of his teachers were all listed under a gallows: Palisander, Kummerkorn, Würfel, Dr. Hochgesang. They were all gone now—peacefully, decease-fully—to their graves. Lichtenberg sat on his third chair. He was writing again. This was about a remedy for hair loss, from which he suffered terribly badly. Thank God it wasn't evident because of the wig. He owned ten of them, no eleven, in various colors and sizes. The hair was of different lengths as well. It contrived to suggest a haircut, where there wasn't much left to cut. He ran his fingers over it, the tips of his fingers. Then he stood up at last. He went over to the door, and let in the girleen, but didn't smile. He was still in his overworld, with words and sentences. He said he could see pictures when he heard words.

Have you seen some now, she asked.

Yes!

She was wearing her bonnet, and looked at him in alarm.

For example, he said, at the sound of people's names. Or the days of the week, for instance "Wednesday." Once he had done a drawing of it.

Of a Wednesday?

Yes.

And what did it look like, your Wednesday?

Lichtenberg took a deep breath and reflected. Because of his hunchback, he had to be clever the whole time, people expected that of him. So you be clever, he told himself, and he looked at the Stechardess, but unfortunately there was nothing forthcoming. So he said what he always said. Well now, he said.

12.

*L*EARNING TO THINK — and read and write — isn't difficult with someone sitting next to you, holding your hand. Or at least sufficiently close to be able to take your hand if you need it. (He doesn't speak, only the hand starts sweating, and is taken away after a while.) And then silence, candlelight, the window propped open. Up in the sky, the moon was running into a cloud, a sprinkling of stars. So that was night! And then another day to come, another one! Lichtenberg couldn't stay in his bed. He was wearing his nightgown, and had something on his head. Later, he slipped into his pink coat, and ran around. Or he pressed an ear to her door, so he could hear her breathing. Then he gussied himself up, as much as possible. That meant the coat with the silver buttons, then, with the tight little sleeves, and the frothing cravat under the chin! He no longer spoke shyly to the Stechardess, he was even rather forward. Well now! he said, and he went up close to her. Then he made a discovery. He discovered she was witty. Hello, he thought, and his brows shot up. He asked: So you want to learn to read?

Yes.

And write?

And write as well!

Then pay attention, you will need to know the following, he said, and explained everything to her. This, he said, is paper, which you write on.

I know!

And this is . . .?

The quill!

With which you . . .?

Scratch!

And this is . . .?

The ink I'm going to splatter everywhere!

Well now, he said.

They wrote either early in the morning, or else by candlelight far into the night. Earlier, he had gone to fetch the spill, now she went to get it. By and by, she had brought all her belongings over to him. There weren't many of them. She had moved in with him one night. Lichtenberg had been wearing the silver wig. He had accompanied the Stechardess. He hadn't got out, though, he had stayed in the coach. He hadn't wanted to meet the parents, least of all the father. He had big heavy hands which scared the little man. He was more or less the same age as himself, just bigger. Often they confronted each other outside the house, and stared at each other in silence. Until Lichtenberg, as the cleverer of them, opened his mouth and said: Yup, that's how it is! Then he looked up at the sky. Both had red-rimmed eyes. Because the father had been drinking, he suddenly put out a hand to touch Lichtenberg's hunchback, and said: You've got something there!

Lichtenberg pushed his hand away and said: I know!

What is it, asked her father, and Lichtenberg said: Nothing much!

And what is it if it's nothing much, he asked again, and Lichtenberg replied: My hunchback!

They had another long pause, then her father asked: And what's it got in it, if I might ask?

Whatever is in a poor human creature, replied Lichtenberg.

I see, said her father. Did you ever have a look inside it, he asked, and Lichtenberg shook his head and said: How can I look inside it? It's sealed!

Well, said the father, you could have maybe . . .

No, said Lichtenberg.

At that he laughed, her father who looked quite different from the little Stechardess, and who had a different sense of humor as well, and he said: Well, well, little sir, well, well! That was too much for Lichtenberg, and he said: Enough already! and he stamped his feet. He didn't like the man, and he pushed away the thought that this was indeed her father. If he saw him coming towards him on the pavement, Lichtenberg either crossed the road, or hurriedly clambered into a coach. Even when he was trying to think of her, that father had a habit of surfacing, and Lichtenberg exclaimed: Not again! Then he said: Enough already! And then the father went away. Now Lichtenberg was sitting in his coach, hoping the Stechardess would quickly leave her family and come to him. In front of him sat the old coachman, with a blanket wrapped round his knees. He held his whip raised, so he could drive off immediately. Well, little gentleman, is she not coming, your daughter, he cried, and Lichtenberg replied: She's not my daughter!

Oh, said the coachman, then what is she? Your granddaughter?

Don't ask so many questions, and draw your curtain so I don't need to see your mug, said Lichtenberg, I need to collect my thoughts!

He stared into the darkness, and thought about this and that. For instance, he thought about his colleagues, and what they were all up to. Picard was in Rome, studying the phosphorescence of quicksilver. Fair enough! Hakus was producing luminescence in vacuums by friction. Just a little bit, anyway! Gray had discovered the transmissability of electricity, and du Fay's great brain had reached the conclusion that electricity existed in two distinct forms. The American Franklin, on the other hand, who wandered through woods and fields with his thick calves, had assumed that there was such a thing as an electrical fluid, and it was this fluid that produced all the symptoms of electricity. Positive and negative electricity were nothing but an insufficiency or an excess of this fluid, that's what the American thought, while Lichtenberg sat at home, waiting for a weighty tome from De Luc, which simply refused to arrive. For unknown reasons, De Luc had broken off his correspondence with him. Was he dead again? (In fact, De Luc hadn't written the work for which Lichtenberg was so anxiously waiting.) And that's how it was with everything. In the drawing rooms of Göttingen, scientific experiments were accounted pretty entertainment. They don't take me seriously, he thought. Well, everyone tried in their own way to get a picture of the world, and to make it conform to their own ideas of it. Lichtenberg was not in a position to confirm the assumption that electricity was a substance. Nor yet was he persuaded that an electrified subject gained weight. Tomorrow I'll pull myself together and write a few lines about its insubstantiality, he thought. He had turned his back on electricity for a long time, but now he would . . .

Outside, a door fell shut in the darkness. The Stechardess, after thirteen years, was leaving the parental home. She had her hands full, and was walking down the street. It seemed that she had grown, and her parents shrunk. She's my girl, he thought, I'll never allow her to go back there again. I'll keep her locked up! She trippled along with short childlike strides, heavily laden. Lichtenberg cried: At last! At last! and ran to meet her. Everything she still owned she was bringing with her: a couple of blouses, a third bonnet, a wooden teddy bear. Lichtenberg called out: I'm coming! and took the bear off her. Then they clambered into the coach, and it whisked them away.

Then she was sitting with him again in his grotto in the Gotmarstrasse. He was wearing his wig. He could feel her warmth through her thin skirt.

Did she want to feel his as well?

With his slightly bent gouty fingers, he could pick up a pen and paper at a moment's notice. He was about to write something again, but just didn't know what.

In the evening, when they had eaten, "this day as well was coming to an end." The Stechardess cleared the table. She folded up the white tablecloth. She fetched first his chair, then hers, and stood them side by side.

Don't trouble, my dear, he said, and she replied: But the chairs won't come by themselves!

Now their supper table had reverted to being a desk. She went and got a couple of cushions for him. They sat there, side by side, and "plunged into the floods of knowledge." "I have made it my rule that the rising sun is never to find me abed," Lichtenberg once wrote. Or: "In the course of a morning's reading, the head will find no end of material!" Then he said: There! and the little Stechard embarked on her reading and writing. Every second or third word he had to help her with. The moon, he said.

That shines, she read.

There was a constant light above them in a constant sky. He jotted something down. "What makes the prospect of Heaven so pleasing to the poor," he wrote, "is the thought of equality."

What did you write just now, she asked.

A truism!

The Stechardess, pretty child, had her bonnet on. It was her sister's. Her sister didn't need it any more, having long since died. The Stechardess read on, a little haltingly. Lichtenberg, plumped up on his cushions, towered below her. Shyly, she smiled down at him. She read a word, then sighed. He needed to help her again. She read a and b and c, which you sometimes sounded like a k, and sometimes like a soft s. After a few days, she could manage whole sentences. She read: The moon! . . .

Come on, he cried, come on!

She took a deep breath, and she read:

> The moon that shines,
> The child that whines,
> The bell that tolls,
> The alderman that . . .

Good, he cried, excellent!

When he had to help her or correct her, she laughed and said: That's what I meant to say! Then she would get stuck again. He rested his hunchback against the table. He didn't spur her on. To take her mind off the strain, he told her a story. In Hanover, he said, he had once spent the night at an inn. His window had overlooked a little lane. It had been fun to watch people's faces change when they set foot in the lane. They thought no one could see them, but he had seen them all. A woman retied her garter, two others pissed crosswise, a third sniggered to himself, a fourth shook his head. A girl was mindful of the night just past, and straightened her hair-band for fresh conquests. And what about you, he asked, have you got a boyfriend.

The Stechardess pressed her lips together, and shook her head.

Won't you tell me, asked Lichtenberg.

I haven't one, she said.

Oh well, he said sadly, I'm sure you'll have one by and by! Or else he told her the story about the yellow trouser button. I don't know, he said, if you ever came across the yellow trouser button, the only metal one I still had. For years he did duty with an admirable tenacity for a button. When I noticed that the service was beginning to tell on him, I employed a new and fashionable button to assist him. Unfortunately, he took it amiss. In December, he started to hang his head, and a fortnight or so later, the bond parted that had held us together for so long, and he lay before me on the floor. I picked up the poor devil, and looked at him one last time. "Thanks," I said, "for your services!" Now I will have to hold my trousers up by myself for the rest of time! And with that he flew into the stream that flows past the house, which I think you know too?

Yes!

Or else he made up a story for her. There is a bird, he said, that knocks holes in the thickest tree trunks. He's very sure of himself. He has so much confidence in his beak, that after every blow, he hops round to the other side of the tree, to check whether he hasn't broken through.

Does he really do that, asked the Stechardess, go round to look?

Don't you believe me?

Not really, she said. What's the bird called?

Professor Kästner, said Lichtenberg with a laugh, you solved that quickly! Was it easy or difficult?

What's easy, and what's difficult, she asked.

To ask that, my child, is easy, said Lichtenberg, to answer it is difficult!

13.

HEN HIS GREAT LOVE came over the little Lichtenberg, he was just investigating electrical friction. "Gilbert, Hauksbee and Guericke discovered it between them," he wrote to Dr. Hufeland, "and I'm sitting at home, awaiting further developments!"

Electrical friction, what was that?

Lichtenberg was standing in his room, wearing his slippers. He had his wig on, and was looking around. Would she come from the left or the right, or would she not come at all? Once again, he hadn't slept much. The day was somewhat advanced. Lichtenberg got into his coat, and looked all over. "I would far prefer," he wrote to Gleim, "to stand in the window with arms crossed, and as soon as enough people had stopped to look at me, I would leap out of my skin!" He was much distracted. Not unpleasantly, though. The Stechardess was with him. Sometimes she was standing in front of him, sometimes next to him, and she had her bonnet on.

Don't worry, she said, I'm not staying!

She was often around him now. Usually, it was to bring him something, a date, a fig, an apple. But often she just wanted to speak to him. What are you doing now, she asked.

I'm looking for something, he said.

And what's the thing called that you're looking for?

I don't know yet.

But how can you know what you're looking for, if you don't know what it's called?

I'll know once I've found it, he said. Then I can give it a name too.

I see, said the Stechardess, and she wanted to help him look for it, and to help him read and write as well. She had made progress. She now understood the words she read, if not always "what was behind them." There is something behind them, isn't there, she asked, or are you making fun of me?

No!

Behind every one of them?

Almost.

And what if there wasn't anything behind them? Tell!

Lichtenberg had his wig on, so that she wouldn't see his worn places so much. As they were now better acquainted, he sometimes took it off. There, he would say, that's enough of that! Or he stroked his skull, and said: And now you see the bare facts! He had rolled up his sleeves, he had hairy arms. The buttons on the cuffs were silver.

Will you show me, she asked, your whatsit? But Lichtenberg said: No! and turned his back to her. Then he moved a little closer to her.

So close, she asked.

He was now often sitting beside her, "inducting her into the sciences." Sometimes he would get a piece of paper, and make a sketch of something for her: an instrument for scratching oneself with, a vessel to put things in, a clamp that held things together. Do you understand, he asked, and she nodded and said: I think so!

It was a bit harder with ideas, because you couldn't sketch those so well.

He tried some anyway. He drew something murky and complicated, and when she asked: And what's that supposed to be? he said: That's Hope!

That is, she said incredulously. He followed her eyes. No, she said, it never is!

All right then, said Lichtenberg, then it's something else! and he pushed the piece of paper away. Sometimes she became quite furious if there was something she didn't understand. No, she said, no one can understand that! I think that's completely incomprehensible! and he took away the piece of paper with Hope on it.

Don't throw it away, I want to keep it! As a keepsake, she said. And when he asked: A keepsake for what? she said: For you! For when you're not alive any more!

He shrank back, and said: Oh! And then: Well, whatever you say!

When she was sitting so close beside him, he was confused and his talk was apt to be muddled. Because "the flow of blood is supposed to be improved by standing," he stood up and ran around. He "didn't have his fingers on the pulse of his sentences," he leapt from one to another. "My head," he wrote to Volta, without mentioning the Stechardess—in all his copious correspondence, he only alluded to her three times, and never once named her—"is not big enough for what lies before me!"

And what lies before you, she asked.

At that time, he wished he could have had his large brown leather suitcase packed, and gone to call on Volta in Parma. Ideally with her, of course, to be able to continue their interrupted scientific conversation with her beside him. But Lichtenberg was not allowed to be seen in public with her. Nor did he have the time for such a long journey. Nevertheless, he often thought about it. Would he stand up to the endless trip—Italy wasn't wide, but it was long!—with his hunchback? Sometimes he gritted his teeth, ran around the block, and called out: I'm going to Italy now!

It never happened.

When he worked, the door had to be locked, he needed solitude. If an idea should come his way, the Stechardess would only bother him. Some things he wanted to set out he forgot in her presence, and others on account of her smell. Where did that come from now? (It came from her skin.) At evening, he cried: I need exercise. Fresh air!

Fresh window air, or street air, asked the Stechardess, and he said: Yes! and was already halfway down the stairs.

Shall I cook you something, she cried.

Yes, he cried, cook, cook!

And what do you want me to cook, she called after him, and Lichtenberg, heart pounding, looked at the ground, and said: I can't stomach very much any more! Things are going downhill with me! I suggest you cook me some gruel.

Salt or sweet, the Stechardess called after him, and Lichtenberg called back: Oh, I don't mind!

And where was he running off to, the little cripple?

A walk! he cried, and shot out of the house.

It was nightingale season, yet again! They sat in the pick of the shrubbery and yelled at him. Lichtenberg was wearing his light coat, it made him less eye-catching in the sunlight. He liked running around in the sun. It'll make me grow, he thought.

He hadn't been out of the house for days. He'd cancelled everything: Lectures, soup-eating, seminars! He had been sitting around thinking at home, and meant to go on thinking to a conclusion. He had failed to welcome Dr. Hufeland, who had made a detour to Göttingen from Hanover in his medical coach, specifically to see him. He had *bolted himself in*. And given him the message: Thank you for thinking of me, you are one of a very few! In spite of that, I am prevented from welcoming you! He had a huge boil in his mouth, and could not speak on account of it. He had, he said, another boil in his brain, and could not think! Another time! he said, and Dr. Hufeland was forced to leap back into his coach and go home. In the matter of his lectures, Lichtenberg sent Müller into the hall, where the students were waiting. He had to tell them: Herr Lichtenberg was hot on the trail of some little thing, or some great business. So leave me alone and push off home! Of course that was a lie. Lichtenberg wasn't hot on the trail of any great business just then. He was sitting at his desk, not working.

Oh? So what was he doing?

He was sitting and listening to the ticking of the time, the mice and the Stechardess. It was as if there was nothing else in the world, and he had to keep thinking about her the whole time. Sometimes he thought of her from a distance, sometimes from up close. He looked in her direction a lot, towards where she had just been. Maybe she was just cooking him something. Maybe she was making him some thick drinking chocolate in her yellow pan. That took a lot of cleaning up afterwards. When the chocolate was ready, she would let it cool down, and call: It's ready! There would be a skin on top that she liked to lap up.

So you've a sweet tooth, said Lichtenberg.

No, she said, a sweet milk tooth!

She would have liked to share the skin with him, but she didn't dare. (They would have to know one another better before she shared her skin with him!) She licked her finger clean. Then she brought in the chocolate. When their eyes met, he lowered his quickly. She smiled, the dear child, while he . . . He was continually writing something down, either in the first, or—"it's more compendious!"—in the third person, or even in the royal we. Everything went into his book. "There is no stranger production than a book," he wrote to Gottfried Hieronymus Amelung. "Set by people who don't understand it, bound by people who don't understand it, sold, read and reviewed by people who don't understand it, generally also written by people who don't understand it . . ."

And what are you writing now, asked the Stechardess, and he replied: Whatever's just going through my head!

And what's going through your head? Tell me! I want to know! Tell!

"In this grammatical fashion, I delineate my fate," wrote Lichtenberg, and snapped his notebook shut. Then he sat down on another chair, and "expelled another article." The name of this one was "On the Construction that is the World," and it was supposed to be about "the lot." But he was distracted. He didn't write what he had intended to write, he wrote the opposite. The construction was too big for him. So he sat down and wrote a thank you letter to Reimarus. "Thank you heartily for your account of the lightning at Osnabrück." Or: "The news of your thunderstorm was very agreeable to me!" Then he went back to the beginning, to nature as such.

And why, asked the Stechardess, don't you write about people?

Ah yes, said Lichtenberg, Nature!

Because that September—to Garre he wrote: "My own September, if God will"—he was always with the Stechardess in his thoughts, he was never on the case. He had his wig on—and how!—but he was distracted. From time to time a thought came along, and he pulled out his notebook, but by the time he had his pen in his fingers, the thought was gone again. That's why Lichtenberg walked about so much. He went down the Wendenstrasse, and looked up at the sky. He wondered whether it would storm where he was. He was scared of storms. Of course he had other fears as well, as for instance fire, lightning, and ghosts. There was already some talk about it among the students, who called him "Doctor Rabbit's Foot." When he was at his lectern, and it started to thunder outside, he forgot what he was going to say. He looked at the heavens and said: Well now! Then he pushed his books and equipment aside and interrupted his delivery. I'm just going to ask them to make me some coffee, he said, you stay here. I'm going to wait until . . . Well, he asked, what do you think I'm going to wait for?

For you to have an idea, called one of them.

I always have ideas, said Lichtenberg, that's not at issue! The issue is what is happening in the heavens! Then he heard further thundering, and he rushed out of the room. Because he had so much imagination, there were many things he was afraid of: poisoned water, ice breaking underfoot, falling down stairs. Thunder and lightning he feared as well. Half his life was behind him already, only he didn't know it. Like most people, he supposed it would all go on indefinitely. When a funeral cart passed him in the town, he shook his head and called: No no, not yet! And he waved it on. Then again, he said, please not forever! That would be too long for me! Sometimes he ran into a neighbor—"We're not really on *friend* terms yet!"—who looked at him with astonishment and asked: Who are you talking to, my dear fellow?

To myself, said Lichtenberg. I am one of those who have plenty to say to themselves!

Then he took out his wastebook, and, with his neighbor peering over his shoulder, he wrote: "While memory lasts, every man is a multitude. The ten year-old, the twenty year-old, the thirty year-old, all go hand in hand with him." Then he put his wastebook away and asked: Did you understand that?

Not really, said the neighbor, and Lichtenberg said: One shouldn't always try and understand everything—where would that get us?

Then both went on their own way.

Even on that day, and with that weather, Lichtenberg was thinking of his love. "Because everything in the world," he once wrote, "is to do with the weather, we just forget it. But it's always with us. It waits quietly in the background, wearing its weather-trousers. It abides an occasion to attack us, because it is there till the end of our days, perhaps longer." There, now I've written enough, he thought, and he snapped his notebook shut.

And now, he thought, what now? Oh yes, he thought, my happiness is outside. He ran up and down the room.

14.

*A*T THAT TIME, Bain-Marie was still running around the house. When she saw the Stech- ardess, she pulled a face and said: What's she doing here? Lichtenberg thought he had to protect her, and he put himself between them. That's enough now! he said, and he packed Bain-Marie off to her room. Leave us alone!

So you want to be alone, do you, Bain-Marie asked ironically.

Yes, alone!

What about her, asked Bain-Marie, I expect she's allowed to stay.

I decide who stays and who doesn't, said Lichtenberg, as he pushed Bain-Marie out the door for the last time. There, he said, now she's gone!

From now on, he was alone with the Stechardess. He had decided on something, you could see it in his eyes. He didn't want to wait any longer . . . He wanted to go up to her, just as soon as darkness fell, and she couldn't see him so distinctly, and declare that he, well, loved her! That he loved her little noddle, her eyes, her breasts.

What, that little man?!

Yes, that little man!

The thought made Lichtenberg come over all peculiar. It's as though they'd cut off all my buttons and my pants were slipping, he thought, but did not write. (He'd already used it.) Then he tossed his wig on top of the cupboard, never to find it again. It wasn't possible to write down everything, there was simply too much of it. Outside it got dark, time for candles.

At that, Lichtenberg's eyes bulged, because his eyesight was even worse in the candle hours. He went up to his window to watch the day fade out over the street. Skin off, half gone, all gone, he thought, and he watched the light disappear. He could hear the Stechardess bustling about. Smells came from the kitchen that made him hungry.

Pst, he thought, pst!

And was that really all he wanted?

From time to time a someone would come walking down the Gotmarstrasse. Lichtenberg watched him go. Both his candles were standing in the depths of his study, so as not to make him visible from outside. Quietly and tinily he stood there, observing the street from his own darkened room. Sometimes, when he thought: Well, now I'm alone! somebody else would appear. His footfall preceded him. Sometimes he would be carrying a lantern, which shed light but also shadow.

Others hummed or whistled to themselves, that way they didn't feel so all alone in the dark. Others again were in a hurry to get home. Once they were gone, their light still flickered for a while, and the echo of their strides ticked on a little. Then it would be all quiet and dark in the Gotmarstrasse again. The man who had just now been whistling was silent, as though a gag had been placed over his mouth. "To do the opposite of something," wrote Lichtenberg, "is also a form of imitation!"

The wealthy Dieterichs were sitting up in their room overhead. They yawned a lot at this time, because as far as they were concerned, the day was done. The servants lugged dishes and plates around. Lichtenberg heard the tinkle. Frau Dieterich was probably overseeing everything, in her green bonnet. Herr Dieterich was smoking his pipe, with a couple of little ones on his knees. Maybe they would have another before long. Lichtenberg could hear little voices from Dieterich's parlor. Or something fell on the floor, with the intention of shattering. But it remained in one piece.

Oh, Stechardess, my dear love, thought Lichtenberg.

For a long time, he had pushed his pleasure in thinking of the girl ahead of him. Now he couldn't put it off any longer. Now it was time!

The Stechardess was in the kitchen, cooking again. The smell went everywhere, even into his glass retorts. Since he couldn't see into the kitchen, he pictured her standing in front of the range. She had her bonnet on. Her tender little ears were covered, but he knew where to find them. The long skirt she was wearing had been passed on to her from her mother. It was so vast, that she had to go through the door sideways, for fear of catching it on something. There was cloth padding on her hips. She liked putting her hands on them, and saying: Look how fat I am! Then she puffed out her cheeks, till she had the face of a fat woman. She owned two pairs of shoes, one brown, one black. When she was wearing the black ones, she shook her head and said: I should have worn the brown ones! What do you think, she asked Lichtenberg, shall I go and change them? Lichtenberg knew she liked messing about with her shoes, and so he replied: Yes, I should! Then she sat down in the changing corner, and changed her shoes. Because of all the padding and stuffing, Lichtenberg didn't really know what her body was like. Was it fulsome or scrawny? Did she have little bosomlets already? Lichtenberg, whose own body had put forth much more in the way of excrescences, often wondered. He leaned against the wall, and looked across at her. Girls' bosoms, he thought, and was quite moved by the thought. They were his loveliest minutes. Well, he said, when he had thought about her breasts for long enough, I'm not sure, but I expect there'll be something there! They've all of them got something!

That evening, she had opened all the windows in her room. Warm wind blowing outside. The criss-crossing streets of her birthplace outside. On the kitchen table lay what they needed for supper: the soup tureen, and two or three plates that already had something in them. One of them had two little apples, the other a lemon. That's how lovingly she's put everything out, he thought. The smell of supper wafted across to him. She had boiled a couple of potatoes for him, he hadn't eaten one yet today. They were being pushed to and fro, and being allowed to steam a while longer. The Stechardess had sat down. The little breeze from the open window tugged at the candle flames. That's what they began by talking about.

It's evening, said Lichtenberg.

Yes, she said, just about.

It's funny if you look out of the window like that!

How come?

Because everything is just about to change, he said, and picked up a crust of bread. That wasn't as binding as the middle. He gnawed at it a little. Then he said: Night. Everything is said to sink into night, but that's not true! We just need to think of water, the lakes, the sea. But that's not presently at issue. We like to think of what isn't there in front of us, it requires us to speculate! Then he reached for the butter-tub, and spread some on his bread. Do you understand what I'm saying?

No.

Well, he said, well! I, for my part, he said, pointing at his bread with his knife, spread it like this! In one corner it's thin. That's where we economize. Then, towards the opposite corner, it's thicker, ever thicker. In that corner, they live off the fat of the land. Till, in the end, while perhaps not exactly a finger-thickness of butter, at least a blade-thickness is spread on it, said Lichtenberg, and pointed once more at his spread piece of bread.

And why do you do that, she asked, spread the butter thickly in one place and thinly in another?

Because, he said, when I'm hungry, I first of all eat everything, even the bit without much butter. Then, when the big hunger is sated, it's the turn of the little one. And for that, I need butter and sausage and cheese, and, why not, ham as well!

Oh, she said, that's how you meant it.

A pause ensued, which they used, as they said, for chomping and slurping.

When the sun's gone down, he said, I don't know if you've observed this too, the world is changed. Even the people are different. In their houses they move closer together and speak more quietly, as though they don't want to be heard. They sit by the stove. The old women cross themselves and sigh a lot. All because of the darkness, better termed blackness, said Lichtenberg, and the pair of them ate. He looked towards the Stechardess and had sinful thoughts, his face turning red. The Stechardess lowered her eyes. Ah yes, he said.

Lichtenberg ate his two potatoes and drank his soup. Then he reached for an evening apple. It was small, but round and juicy. Lichtenberg sniffed at it a bit. Because he had just been talking about seeing, he now turned to smelling.

Do you remember yesterday's apple, he asked the Stechardess.

It's already behind us!

It was bigger, but just as round!

That's true.

There are round and hard and half-wizened ones.

What are you saying?

That there are various versions of apples too, said Lichtenberg. We roll them across the table, and we cut them open, but we never look into their souls!

Apples? Or are you referring to people?

Both, said Lichtenberg. The one is attached to his family, the other to a branch. They both spread their respective aromas, and Time has got his tooth in both of them. There, he said, and reached for his knife. If it wasn't silver, then it had to be steel. He cut out the core, first the left half, then the right. Then he peeled both parts.

Do you still want me to watch, or am I allowed to go on eating, asked the Stechardess.

You may go on eating!

And what were you really trying to say?

You're right, my child, said Lichtenberg. There is nothing in common between a human creature and an apple core!

Then they finished eating their bread and butter, and their meat and their apple. He drank wine, and she drank bouillon. And Lichtenberg was still no further with his seduction. Oh Lord, he thought, how can I get the girl to love me?

But why should she?

Then a thought common to lots of ugly and sensitive men: At least she could close her eyes and let me love her! Normally, now, he would have crossed into the big room with her, and sat down opposite her with lots of room between them, but that wouldn't have helped either. If I put out my fingers—he had scrubbed them with soap—to touch her, she'll run out of the room, he thought. And I'm not able to catch her, my legs aren't long enough! So let's go to the experimenting room, it stinks of science there, but at least we'll have a few more ideas!

Isn't it a bit cramped in there?

Lichtenberg shook his head. No, it's just right, he said. Our arms and legs and other bits might bump into each other from time to time, but what harm would that do?

What other bits are you talking about now?

Oh, said Lichtenberg, just those intestines and those twiddly bits, and he went next door.

The Stechardess still had a bit of tidying up to do, and then she followed.

Isn't it strange how quickly she comes, he thought, if it had been a handsome young man one could understand it, but it's only me! She sat down in the corner where the retorts and dishes were standing. At first Lichtenberg had wanted to drag her. But she came all by herself, tweaking at her skirt, and saying: My skirt!

Pretty, said Lichtenberg. Then they sat there, and after the time of staring came the time of touching. Before this they said one or two words, well, what do you think? About the warmth of their own body and that of the other. It went like this.

What would you say, he asked, how many candles are needed to turn a dark room into a light one?

Maybe three?

And a cold one into a warm one?

A warm one?

Yes, like this! The sweat is running down my brow. There, he said, and he wiped it, and his finger was a little damp. We should blow out some of the candles, he said.

Would you like me to?

Yes, blow them out!

The Stechardess stood up. She went over to the candles and blew two of them out.

How many shall I leave, she asked. Two or three?

One, said Lichtenberg.

The Stechardess blew out all the candles except one. That one flickered a bit. Now there was half-dark, and there was silence for a long time, until Lichtenberg suddenly pulled himself upright and called out: A dress, a dress!

You keep changing the subject, she said. What are you talking about now?

A dress, he exclaimed, a dress!

What dress are you talking about?

None in particular, said Lichtenberg, a dress per se. I was wondering . . .

Yes?

What it feels like to wear a dress!

No different to anything else.

No no, said the cripple, a man's coat feels completely different. A girl's dress is lighter.

You'd like to touch it, wouldn't you, asked the Stechardess.

Why not, said Lichtenberg, and he confessed: He had always longed to touch the dress of a girl or woman, only none had ever let him. "There is" he said, "a virginity of the soul with girls, and a moral devirgination; with many, it happens very early, but they're still afraid of it." Then he wiped his hand clean on his trousers, and touched her beautiful dress. It wasn't the first time. He had quite often, in passing or "accidentally" touched her like that, but each time he had apologized, and she had said: That's all right! And then she'd forgotten all about it. Whereas now he knew he was touching her, and she knew it too. First he touched her left sleeve, then her right. He had to breathe hard, it was very exciting for him. So that was her little sleeve, that was her shoulder, that was her hand!

My God, he said.

After that, they sat around again, now he had her hand in his. The Stechardess sat stiffly and silently, as though it wasn't her hand. As though it was someone else's altogether.

Sometimes they get a bit sweaty, she said, and Lichtenberg said: Oh! Well, he said, as long as there's sweat, there's life. There are other ways of telling, too, like if the heart's beating!

I know!

Yes, the heart!

Oh, said the Stechardess, I'd as soon not think of that! When it stops beating, that'll be it, and I'll be laid out on the big bed. They'll fold my hands over my belly, and lower me into the ground like my little brother they were going to christen Hans. Now he doesn't have a name. Shortly afterwards, another one came along to whom they gave the name Hans, because it was available, and because my parents had fixed on it. He's still alive, but in America, so he might as well be dead! And then: Please stop!

What am I doing?

Your hand! Where you're putting it!

Then Lichtenberg took a deep breath and asked: Where is your heart? Will you let me feel it! and still he was holding her hand. She pretended not to be aware of anything, and he asked: Up a bit or down a bit?

More in the middle, she said. I think it's skipping about!

And where is it skipping now?

More up now, I think.

May I touch it, asked Lichtenberg. May I count the strokes?

Oh God, she said, you'd better not!

But I'll be very careful!

Oh God, she said, go on then! Oh God, so long as you do it very lightly!

They were now sitting very close together, the strange couple, in the large university apartment, as though they were afraid of the darkness. They were surrounded by jars and retorts and pans, all his scientific appurtenances. And then all his many books of course! Some were lying on their backs, others on their fronts. When they looked out of the window, they saw the stars. Did they actually twinkle? That night, Lichtenberg was unable to reach a conclusion.

There was no one around on the street. No one looking up at them. Everyone was at home. A good many had gone to bed, and were staring up at their respective ceilings. A few might already be asleep. Others were dying. It has to be some time, they thought, it just happens to be now! Or they were caught up in some dream or other. (Maybe their dying was a dream.) In their dream, they had become something else that they were dragging around with them: some enmity, a quiet conversation, something that oppressed them. They were taken out of their lives for half a night. How sad it all is, thought Lichtenberg, and rubbed his hunchback. Then he thought: What the heck, I'll give it a go! and he grabbed her breast.

Oh God, said the child, you mustn't! and he replied: Oh God, I know!

Oh God, she said, and she took a deep breath, and Lichtenberg said: I'll be gentle with you! And he waited a moment and asked: And will you be gentle with me too?

Yes, she said, I will too!

Then, after a pause—a pause for reflection, as it might be— they laid their hands on each other. Lichtenberg touched her on her throat and her shoulder and finally on her breast, the Stechardess touched him on his cheek and his face. That went on for a little while. A couple of times she said: I'd better go to my room now, meaning the one where she slept. He kept saying: No, not yet!

She said: Yes, I have to go to my room!

And he: Stay! Please stay!

Just a moment longer then!

All right, just a moment!

And then he slowly undressed his little girl, his heavenly bride, his other half, the ray of light on his horizon, etc. He sensed, no: he felt . . . "There is no more fatuous person than the man describing his feelings, especially if he has a little prose at his command." First he untied her apron, and threw it on the floor. He had never yet undressed a girl, he needed to learn how it was done. But she had never been undressed by a man either, and she didn't notice how clumsy he was. She thought it had to be like that, and she said again: Oh God! Finally, he had ripped everything open and tossed it on the ground, and he felt her bare skin. He brushed over it, first with his fingertips, then with the whole of his hand.

Don't hurt me, she said.

Then she helped him to lift her out of her skirt and out of her peculiar underpinning. He gave it a little push, and it rolled across the floor. Under her dress, she was minute. Her breasts were hardly worth mentioning. They hadn't yet begun. When she was finally naked, and he pulled her to him, he saw she was still a child. She got quite beside herself, throwing her little head from side to side and crying: No! No! He said: Wait! and blew out the last candle.

What happened next was the laborious, brutal and bloody business!

They would both have given up, only they were too far along already. There was no going back. They lay in the fourposter bed, feeling lost. Now the Stechardess pulled him to her, now she pushed him away again. Then she cried: Please leave me! No! and he was about to obey, but then she said: I don't mean it! Stay! She was appalled and fascinated and wouldn't have minded crying. She was terrified of his hunchback, which she stroked, and of the brutal thing he had between his legs and kept attacking her with. It went on for a long time.

15.

*L*ICHTENBERG, O LICHTENBERG, what's happened to you? No one's cracked a joke, but you're smiling again!

There he was lying on his back, breathing deeply, sometimes in, sometimes out. His eyes were closed. He had to keep his mouth open, "so as not to suffocate for happiness." "I was looking," he wrote, "neither to left nor right, just then I was looking in!" In spite of everything he had just experienced— he had found limitless fulfilment— he was still the same man, too bad, too bad! He was still runtish and hunchbacked, his head was still too big for his body. His nose was still in the same unfortunate place, his chin, his eyes, the lot. Even the teeth . . . No, we're not going to talk about the teeth! He was back in his nightcap, a little sweaty, admittedly, but . . . "Maybe I could make a successful lover, in spite of my ugliness," he wrote later. "I know how repugnant it must be to embrace me. I thank God I am without shame!" That's why he even let her see his hunchback, naked as God—was it God?—had made it. He lay on his right side under the canopy, his limbs sprawled. The canopy, thought Lichtenberg, is green, because I find it restful. The bed was a little bit messy. It came to life at night. ("It creeps and crawls," he said.) It was the faithful old vermin that had been sharing his bed with him for a long time. God knows where they went in the daytime. Some of them he heard, and some he felt on his skin. It was worst towards morning, that's when the Göttingen cockroaches came out. With their long thin legs they scrabbled around above Lichtenberg's head. Sometimes one of them would lose its grip and fall on top of him, and snatch him from his dream. He swore a bit in Latin, and brushed the cockroach away. He looked towards the window, from where he was expecting the new day.

Are you asleep, he asked the little Stechardess.

No, she said, are you?

I'm not either!

Did you sleep?

No, he said, and you?

I didn't either!

Certainly, there could be no question of sleep on that night. When it finally got light—he would devote a couple of lines to the matter of sunlight, either today or tomorrow—the cockroaches would disappear again. He wondered where.

Oh, happy Lichtenberg!

He wasn't wearing much. He would henceforth cease to conceal his infirmity. He was a man like any other. He was . . . In fact, he wasn't wearing anything, but you couldn't see that. He had pulled the summer coverlet up over his knees, up to his penis. Half of it was showing, and it was an impressive half. Oh God, he sighed, and was, so to speak, happy. At last he was no longer alone in bed.

Oh, Lichtenberg you lucky roach!

It was still September, but not for much longer! The color of the sky was . . . Nor is anything known of the color of the wallpaper, or the stuffing of the thick pillows. The weather . . . It was dark, too early to say. By his side lay the beautiful child. She was all curled up, she was almost as small as he was. Had she gone back to sleep? She was naked under the covers, maybe she had allowed herself to be undressed. Her clothes were tidily folded up: the long dress and the bonnet and the corset and the white shift. Everything in a neat pile. Her shoes were under the chair that Professor Kästner always sat on when he held forth about his earthquakes. To date, he had experienced and recorded no fewer than seven of them, so that mankind would never forget them. If he was lucky, he could expect to live through another five, making a round dozen. Lichtenberg had only experienced one, and had stolen the others from Kästner. He kept them locked up in his desk drawer, so that they wouldn't fall into the wrong hands. Then he heard the Stechardess breathing again next to him, and he wondered: Did she want to sleep some more?

He asked: Do you want to sleep some more?

No, do you?

I don't either, he said. He wanted to think some more, but not about people, he didn't need them today. He thought about the sound his thoughts made when they emerged freshly from his head. Then he thought of the scraping of his pen, from which something always flowed—a whole world when things were going well. He thought about the wooden stairs in his house, and about his friend Erxleben coughing and spitting. Finally he thought of the miracle quack Philadelphia, who had turned up in Göttingen with his retinue. Philadelphia affected a tricorn hat on his head and green gloves. He spoke only English, or so he claimed anyway. He was long and lean like all liars, and had announced on the Zindelstrasse that he would demonstrate his miracles now in Göttingen as well. But then along came Lichtenberg. With Dieterich's help he had had something else printed up overnight, and posted all over town. Now one could read that the miracle quack would "throw himself head first, hands tied, from the loftiest church tower in the town without sustaining any injury." All were cordially invited to view the spectacle. But nothing came of it. Before anyone could feast their eyes on the miracle, Mr. Philadelphia had left town again, in the middle of the night. Apparently, he didn't want to leap onto the Göttingen cobbles head first after all.

Lichtenberg, o Lichtenberg, you happy fantast!

In the index of a book about him, *happy* is listed as *see under: happy go lucky*. (Straight afterwards comes the word *health*.)

What about Lichtenberg's happiness? His happy-go-luckiness? If it was ever to come about, it was high time. There are various entries in his wastebooks on the matter of *happiness*. For instance, there is: "To feel again a happiness to which we have become inured, we need only to imagine that we had lost it, and only found it again at that moment." Or there is: "A long happiness loses by its duration." Or: "Upsetting, that one can go too far in the investigation of these things." He himself was a case in point. He wished he hadn't gone so far in his endeavor to research the human heart.

What a morning, that morning! How they hoked and hunkered together so tightly. How far beside themselves they were! The very circumstance that such a night should be followed by such a morning! Heaven and earth were still quiet, but *chez* Lichtenberg they were talking again, and everything would go on as before. Then it was as though nothing had happened, as though nothing could possibly have happened. Lichtenberg began to despair again. He didn't think he could ever be happy. He didn't think he would ever make a discovery or an invention that would "immortalize" him, "render him deathless," "carry his name through the centuries and the millennia." When it comes down to it, he thought, I have nothing to say! He had overestimated himself. He would have to begin all over again. He would consecrate himself to a new field, for instance the nerves of frogs.

Professor Galvani in Bologna, he said, has established that . . .

The Stechardess pulled the covers over her tiny breasts. Do you still love me, she asked.

Of course I do!

In short, Galvani had established that by applying an electric current to the ganglia of a dead frog, one would elicit twitchings from it. Galvani put on his spectacles and walked up to the beast. He saw the dead thing live again. Move, at any rate. He concluded he had discovered a type of "animal electricity," and wrote to tell them all about it: Müller von Itzehoe, Johann von Zimmermann, Herschel, Dr. Blumenthal, everyone. When Lichtenberg got his letter, he shook his head, and did his own experiments. His work room and kitchen were soon jammed with dead frogs that were supposed to move. Instead, they started to stink. He was loath to throw away the expensive frogs, though, maybe one or other of them would still twitch. Lichtenberg asked himself: Why is it that some twitch and others . . .? The Stechardess lay on her side of the bed. She wanted to talk again. She had pulled the sheet over her little breasts so that he couldn't see them. (He would see them often enough.)

You have to lecture today, don't you, she asked.

Yes.

Is it true that you take your pointer and stand in front of them?

That sounds possible!

And that you always begin with a question? With the question: "Now, gentlemen, what is Nature?"

Not always.

But sometimes?

Yes, sometimes.

And do they know the answer?

No.

And do you tell them, she asked. Tell me! Do you tell them? Say!

After that night, Lichtenberg was slow to return to the world. When he finally had returned, he took his pen and pressed it into her hand. There, he said, write it down before it gets lost like so much else! and she wrote: "The most important things in the world flow through tubes."

Through what?

That's right, said Lichtenberg. Then he took the pen away from her again.

And what will you do now, asked the Stechardess, and Lichtenberg replied: Now it's beginning all over again.

What is?

The daily grind, he said, what did you think? Then they looked out of the window, and truly, it was already light. He stood in a corner, and pulled on a white shirt and grey trousers. Followed by this and that, "none of it essential, but dictated to us by the fashion of our day." Now, he said, the man is dressed and wants his coffee!

Does he want it strong or weak?

Strong, said Lichtenberg, so that the man doesn't shrivel up!

That day the man didn't shrivel up. He felt like a new man. With a new confidence, he stood and looked about him and observed . . . The silence, the air, the birds! At breakfast, he gestured to a chair, and had her sit down close by him. Yes, he said, this is where I want you, always!

After that came the strengthening repast, and the learned little man helped himself liberally to "get his stomach in gear and so recover his strength." He ate thick slabs of bread and butter with red and yellow jams and . . . . Well, his apple of course! Everything, it appeared, was favorable and to hand. When he dropped a book and picked it up, it was open at a place he had been looking for for a long time.

Look at that, he said.

How he had longed for that place, how he was eaten up with longing for it! "Months, if not longer!" He had thought the place was lost for all time.

Look what a wonderful scholar I am, he said to the Stechardess. He was moved almost to tears.

When she asked: What is it? he replied: You bring me luck! Something is found that was lost for a long time.

He took the open book into a corner and decided to go through the place with fresh strength and try to *incorporate it*, if he could, clandestinely in some weak point of his own work. Love gave him hope for his scientific endeavors too. Look at how I'm getting ahead, he said, everything's going to be different from now on! He needed to get out into the fresh air, even if it was just a step or so outside the front door. He was already shod, now he put his wig on. Then he tied his stock, then inserted his silver tiepin. He had the urge to talk to someone about his "undeserved good fortune"—by which he meant not just the place in the book he had found again, but the Stechardess as well. He ran out of the house. Even though it was early still, he ran round to Erxleben's. He should have stayed at home!

16.

IS OLD—STILL YOUTHFUL—friend had recently moved into the Zindelstrasse, very close to Lichtenberg. When Lichtenberg slipped into his slippers and stood by the window, they often saw one another and waved across the street. Dr. Erxleben, standing on the ground floor, thus a little further down, seemed to be reaching up for something that eluded his grasp. The poor fellow, thought Lichtenberg, shutting the window again. That moment, Erxleben began coughing again, and disappeared into the depths of his room. Probably he was going to write something down. He was a scientist as well. He was often leafing around in books, appearing to wait for something to happen. When Lichtenberg passed his house, he would shout up to him, and for ten minutes they would discourse on scientific subjects, as for instance the new camera obscura, which imitated the human eye. With great effort—and at great expense—Erxleben had fitted out his new house, and, as he said, *for the duration*. All the furniture and the beds and the pictures were now standing or hanging in the places where they belonged, for Erxleben "to whom love had smiled" had gotten himself hitched. Lichtenberg had been very helpful to him over this. He had put on his wig and gone around with him a lot. He said: This way! and introduced him into various houses. Often Riekchen, his fiancée, would be of the party. She would trot along between them, and Erxleben would ask: Is this all right, or are we walking too fast for you?

Riekchen would look at him worriedly and say: I'm all right, but what about you? Then they knocked on a door, and Lichtenberg, who was known to all Göttingen, would introduce the young couple as "his good friends"—or sometimes: "my only friends." Evening was approaching, the sky was getting in disguise. The gentlemen took off their hats. The young bride was given pride of place, and had to sit down first. Then a bottle of wine was uncorked, and a toast was drunk to "the happy event." Erxleben had his arm around her shoulder, and was coughing with happiness. When the wedding day itself arrived, Lichtenberg put on his prettiest little coat. He put on his wig and went to the wedding, though a confirmed non-dancer. There was laughing and crying and eating and drinking aplenty. Lichtenberg's little coat was so subtly tailored that his two humps were invisible. They really are, he thought, and in front of the mirror he turned this way and that, he cut them out, those superfluous humps, the magician! At any rate, that day he believed they were no longer visible. He scuttled around the bride a lot, and kept looking at her from every conceivable vantage point. Sometimes he dropped something on the floor, and had to bend to pick it up. And then he would inspect her from below as well. After the wedding feast they had to put him in a sedan chair and carry him the few yards home, because "he had looked too deeply into various glasses."

And now?

Now he was standing at the door, but there was no sign of Erxleben. Only his young wife and a few strangers stood there and looked at him. There were carriages parked before and behind, with mourning ribbons. The young Madame Erxleben had covered her mouth with her white hand. Lichtenberg shrank back. He remembered how that night—their night—he had heard noise outside, and a knock at the door. He hadn't got up to answer it though, he had had better things to do. Then the knocking had stopped, and he had forgotten all about it. Now he saw the young woman, and he wanted to feel some emotion, but he couldn't. The feelings he had wanted to have at the time only came along much later. They were pure horror. By the time he could finally look Madame Erxleben in the eye, he knew everything, and had completely frozen. Even as he had been "encountering the highest, wholly unscientific heights of his life as a man, the highest bliss of a man's life," his friend Erxleben had died among paroxysms of coughing.

Now it was early morning. Doctor Lichtenberg was wearing his lime-green tunic. On his feet he had a pair of yellow shoes. He had experienced complete happiness as a lover, and he wasn't allowed to be happy! Fate, always on the lurk, had struck while he had been looking away! His friend, his most excellent friend!

Madame Erxleben stood with a couple of workmen in front of the house they had only recently purchased. The workmen clambered around the frontage, putting up black mourning ribbands. Madame Erxleben had her arm raised, and was pointing out the places where she wished the ribbands to be fixed. Yes, up there, she said. One of them propped a ladder against the wall. He took off his cap. Then he put it back on again. The other passed him the mourning ribbands they were to affix to the windows. Now it was a house in mourning. So this was the way it had been: While Lichtenberg had been lying with the little Stechardess in the fourposter, Erxleben had been coughing and spitting himself to death in his room. Lichtenberg put his arm round the shoulder of the young widow. He clenched his fist. He brandished it against the heavens—yes, just like that!—as though he wanted to threaten someone up there, probably the Almighty in person. Then they went into the house together. In the dark, he almost tripped over something. It was Erxleben's coffin. It was still empty, however. The lid was balanced precariously against the wall. Lichtenberg gave it a wide berth. He thought of his friend's life and wondered if that was it for him.

Yes, that was it!

A little old woman ran around, squirting the place with rose water. Lichtenberg put his fist to his mouth, and bit it gently. Thank God Madame Erxleben was pregnant! Thrown out of one emotion into another, Lichtenberg allowed her to clasp hold of him. And so they gave each other support. Then there was something else she had to do outside, and she left him in the house of death alone. He drew breath and looked around. This was where he would be displayed! Lichtenberg climbed the stairs, and went into the coughing man's room.

He lay dead on the big bed where he had previously lain with his wife. Lichtenberg tugged at his wig, and approached his friend. Because he had passed on, Erxleben had stopped coughing. He seemed somehow menacingly heavy and silent. His head was a weight. Everything pressed down towards the earth which now wanted Erxleben back.

Lichtenberg sighed and said: Oh dear!

Erxleben's legs were heavy, also his shoulders and arms, but most of all . . . Well, his head. Never in all his life had Lichtenberg seen such a heavy head. Lichtenberg would have liked to lift it up, but then he let it be. He walked round his friend. Because he was still tired from his night of love, he propped himself on Erxleben's desk as he passed. That was the position in which he always reflected, before committing something to paper. And that was how it was now. Confronted with the death of his old, newly-married friend, though, nothing came to mind. He wanted to remember what he had last talked about with him, but he couldn't remember. All things leave the world doubly, he thought, and wanted to write down the fine thought, but then he felt too squeamish to sit down beside the dead man and write. Oh, he thought, Devil take it, and all the rest of it!

Erxleben's nose had gotten pointed, and was getting more and more pointed. The position of his head was now how it would remain for all time. Since the time he had last seen him, Erxleben seemed to have become not only thinner but also smaller. Curious, thought the word-collector, he looks more significant than usual as well! That was it! Erxleben had gained significance after his death, as though he had taken a second doctorate at the University. His face seemed narrower, and the brow pressed down more massively on the nose. Oh Lord, what are these thoughts you're thinking when you've just experienced the apotheosis of your own life, thought Lichtenberg. You'd do better to go home!

The corpse women went around silently. They filled the anteroom. Erxleben's house, still unpaid for, that would now have to be vacated and returned, began to change as well. Nothing remained in its appointed place. The furniture was in front of the wrong walls. That way there would be enough space for all the people who would come to say their goodbyes tomorrow. A lot had already been carted away. Lichtenberg looked once more at his poor, forever coughing and now silent friend. He had coughed his last! Then the corpse women pushed Lichtenberg out the door, saying: We're not done yet!

Who would be, said Lichtenberg.

He went down the stairs, one at a time. On the ground floor he hurriedly tiptoed round the back of Madame Erxleben, out of the house and across the street, into his own house, where there was a girl waiting for him, to whom he had to give a quick kiss.

17.

THAT DAY, THE TWO OF them shut their windows and doors, and huddled together. If someone knocked, they didn't answer. Even though the Stechardess had never met Dr. Erxleben, Lichtenberg had to tell her about him. He had to tell her how long they'd been friends, what he had looked like, what he used to wear. They were sitting side by side, and he was holding her hand. After a while, they got back to the other subject, from death back to life. They forgot the man in the house next door, and crawled nearer to one another. They decided they didn't really need all those big rooms, and they preferred to remain in just one, and the smallest one of all. That was the one that had the bed in it, to which they were now powerfully drawn. After dinner, when his belly was full, he cried: Let's go and lie down! and they undressed one another, each in his own way. Lichtenberg tossed everything onto the floor, the Stechardess picked it all up again. She made tidy little piles, until he got impatient, and cried: Come on! You can do that later! Then they crept in together and looked at each other rapturously, because there was so much to look at. They pressed their cheeks together, so that they could feel those too. Each felt the warmth of the other, and his flesh and the bones underneath. And of couse that was nice!

Now he was doubly near to her, and when she asked: How? he said: Firstly by rubbing my skin against yours, and secondly . . .

Yes?

. . . by explaining my science to you! You do want to understand about it, don't you?

Oh, so that's what you meant!

And so he drew her into his life and into his thoughts. Sometimes he would lie next to her, and speak across to her. Sometimes he spoke up to her. Ever since she'd known that she was permitted to ask questions, she asked questions all the time. She went up to a brass pulley and asked: What's this? He told her quickly. And this, she asked, pointing to a pendulum machine for the measurement of gravity. And he told her about that too.

I see, she said, and he said: Well, now you know everything!

Not quite, she said, a bit more than I did!

Then they smiled again, and sighed out of the fullness of their feelings. Their feelings were in their hearts. He got out her little breast, and asked: Do you mean in here? and she said: Stop that, you're making me blush! When he wanted her with him, she had to drop whatever she was doing, and come to him straightaway.

You mean right now, she asked, and he nodded and said: Yes, right now!

Sometimes, very curious this, she would suddenly start crying. He sat there awkwardly. What's the matter with you, he asked.

Oh, she said, just leave me be!

It often happened in front of the window, with the weather and the time of day.

And why do you do it, he asked, I mean the thing with the tears? and she said: I don't exactly know. I think it's because of happiness.

I see, said Lichtenberg.

Sometimes he sent her into the kitchen, he wanted to be alone at the window. But there wasn't much to look at. Often he could spend a whole morning there, and not see anyone beyond a farmer's wife or a market woman carrying something in a basket. She would be so wrapped up that you couldn't see much of her, except her head and her knees. It wasn't exactly cold, but it was cool. Lichtenberg hadn't started having fires lit yet. He himself was all aglow. He heard his girl in the kitchen or the corridor. Should he run out to her? Or should he wait for her to come to him, and then make plans together? Because they were at home the whole time, she wanted to go off somewhere. Once, she said: Out into the big wide world!

Yes, he said, and stroked his humpback, we'll go away somewhere!

Where to, asked the girl.

Where d'you think, he said, I told you!

Yes, but what part of the world? Aren't there lots of them?

Lichtenberg smiled and thought about it. If he said: We'll go out into the world, she'd be happy with that. They wouldn't even have to go. For a long time he didn't say anything. The narrow Gotmarstrasse, the whole country, the wide world were all going through his head. Then he finally took a deep breath and spoke the magic word that hadn't gone through his head for long time now: Italy!

What?

Italy!

Oh, said the Stechardess, so that's what you meant!

Yes, said Lichtenberg, and with his hands he formed a couple of hills and a bit of beach the way they apparently have in Italy, the sort of scent that wafted around there. Yes, he said, that's Italy for you!

The sun had only just risen, and now it was already setting again. They were hunkered on the garden seat together, the cripple and the girl. They had put their hands together. Or else he laid his scholar's hand on her little tit, but ever so gently. Sometimes she took his hand off and said: You really shouldn't or: Not now!

Why not now?

Somebody could see!

But there's nobody here!

Yes, she said, that's true!

They put their hands together again. His were always cold. He gripped hers tightly, but she held his too. She waited to see if he would say or do anything else, but for a long time that was it. Then he made an extravagant movement and began to speak. He painted a picture for her of the world that he wanted to live in with her, hills and forests and vineyards "and all the stuff behind that you can't see from the distance." Not much longer now!

Then what?

Our trip together!

A trip?

A trip!

Yes, they would go on voyages! Oh, how strange! No sooner had they met, than they were in a hurry to leave! He took her little hands and placed them on his head, "which is where all those things are that don't exist!" Then he told her about Italy. He knew it well, if only from books, because he had never been there either. He often went for walks in the short, narrow lanes, but only in books, which he "leafed through full of wistfulness and longing." That was where he wanted to be!

Who with?

Well, who do you think!

He had his eyes closed, and conjured up everything in front of her. He talked about the mild climate, and how much good it would do them both. He even told her about his financial situation. It was such as to permit him to visit the mild, warm country with her quite soon. He had a little money, "that he had scraped together with all fours over the centuries." He kept it—"pst, not a word!"—in their big bed, she just hadn't known about it before. It was under the mattress in a leather bag. This bag, Lichtenberg explained, was in a place that no one would be able to find, but he would show it to her before long. Then he kissed her, and began to rave all over again. For years he had been thinking of Italy, saving up for Italy, "held conversations with himself" about Italy, and now the time had come! He even dreamed in Italian! They would leap into a coach—yes, leap!—and move to Italy, the grease was already on the wheels. The money he had was more than they needed for food and drink and oats and axle-grease. Also, he was full of courage, and, well, health, and then of course he had her to sit next to him on the long journey and hold his hand. For the sake of appearances, lest anyone think any ill of them, they would take his old university friend, the Danish Financial Counselor Ljungberg with them, to be their *chaperon*. He would sit in front with the coachman, and she would be inside with him. Or he would stick her in a man's coat and trousers, so that everyone would take her for his brother. She wouldn't be able to talk much on the journey, because otherwise people would begin to suspect because of her high voice. The coachman would be in on the plan from the beginning, he would be bribed with a few pennies. If we take a look at the calendar, said Lichtenberg, we have precisely nine weeks in which to get ready. No one, if humanly possible, should live without having seen Italy for themselves, it's good for the body and the spirit! Or are you scared, child, of going on such a long journey with me?

No.

Not even in winter?

Not ever!

On that day—this was a conversation they then had quite often—Lichtenberg would stop at this point. Then he began all over again. He wanted it over and over again before he set out. (In the end, they never made it to Italy, neither of them. In the end, they would have been nowhere together, except in their rooms!) Lichtenberg had his hand on her knee. He rubbed it a bit. Because he didn't get much exercise—basically, all he did was trot back and forth between bed and lecture room—he would start sweating readily. He sat there now with his handkerchief, held it aloft, and said: Look, wet! Then he asked: Where had we got to? and the Stechardess replied: A foreign country! and he said: Oh yes, Italy! The time to see Italy is autumn or winter, when it isn't so hot. We'll wear sensible, loose-fitting clothes so that our skin can breathe.

Me too?

Yes, you too! We'll leave the Göttingen winter behind. We'll put on our straw hats and go walking under blossoms.

In winter?

Yes, in winter! While everyone else is creaking up and down the Kurze Geismarstrasse with icicles in their beards, we'll slip out of our coats, and run around in shirtsleeves. Do you know why?

No.

We'll be sunning ourselves, child. Bitter oranges will be growing by the roadside. If you fancy eating one, you'll have only to put out your hand.

For a bitter orange?

Of course. What else?

When Lichtenberg sat there and talked like that, the Stechardess got big round eyes. Sometimes she took his hand and held it up to her cheek. Sometimes she would say something as she did so, something like: Sweetie-pie! or: My Lord! She hadn't yet seen anything of the world, and how could she have? She imagined something completely different, something altogether more wonderful than the real thing. He let her tell him about it, it cast a spell over his own world. Sometimes she got up and sighed and was full of joy and expectation. She ran into the little kitchen. She stood in front of the stove. They had got rid of Bain-Marie, and now everything was sparkling and tidy. Come on, my little bear, she said, sit down on your little stool! It's a bit higher than mine is. We'll eat in a moment, and then you can go on talking!

Do I talk too much for you?

In the early time—at the beginning of their *marriage sauvage*—Lichtenberg still had his wig on a lot. He sat next to her. Sometimes he said: Just a tick! and went around the block. In Göttingen, by daylight, he was instantly recognizable. He was now wearing a pink shirt, his silver wig—"it makes me look more distinguished"—and his . . .When he had spoken about something difficult in the lecture hall, he always wanted to "go out for a breather" at noon. He always had a book in his hand that he could browse in. Rarely was he without. Sometimes he wanted to be alone, and then he said: And now I'd like a bit of peace from you all! Then he went "to keek at his girl, and from very close to." They leaned against each other, and he said: Aah! That wasn't yet satisfaction, but even so! When she asked: Was I near enough to you? he replied: No! and drew her *even nearer.* He had taken up his scribbling again, and always carried his wastebook around with him. He sat down, opened it on his knee, and asked: What do people say when they want to be left alone? and she said: "Give me peace!" and he said: Just so! and wrote something down in his book. He wrote: "If, for certain reasons, he is unable to work and gradually feels ashamed of himself, he will occasionally, to friends, claim another's work as his own. Occasionally also he will insert another's sentence in amongst his own." Then he put the book away again, and sat down at her table-lay-thyself! There, another sentence is in the bag! he said, and surveyed what was on the table. Because of his poor eyesight, he always pulled his plate very near at mealtimes. He only ate what he could quite clearly see, and he only saw what he wanted. The rest he preferred to sniff at, and then push away.

Ever since the Stechardess had been sitting beside him at table, he was eating less. The hunchbacked little fellow was thinking about his appearance. He wanted to be svelte and youthful. Well, his belly got less, but the man didn't grow any taller! When he had helped himself to something from this dish and that dish and had begun to eat, he would suddenly exclaim: Oh! and push it away again.

But you haven't eaten anything yet!

I don't need anything more, he said, I'm full up! Then he took a match from his coat and picked his teeth. Everything had ridden up in front of him. Alongside his half bottle of wine, she had put this and that. Along with the slice of beef now two instead of, as once, five potatoes. She had "put out their eyes," and peeled and boiled them. All right, then, he would eat two! He pushed the pudding away and said: We can have that another day! It's too much for me today!

What about me, she asked, can I eat something sweet?

Yes, eat! You need to grow!

The evening was when the time of light was succeeded by the time of darkness. It marched up the Gotmarstrasse and slowly turned the corners.

At last, there it is, he cried.

The Stechardess was sitting opposite him, smiling at him. She wasn't wearing her bonnet, her forehead was exposed. Lichtenberg stroked it with his fingertips, and she said: Smooth, isn't it?

She will never be more beautiful as long as she lives, he thought, and ate a couple of spoonfuls of herring salad.

That was on another day. Or else he ate a couple of sardines with some apple that she'd sliced finely. He speared a piece, laid a bit of sardine on top of it, and shoved it in his mouth. He said: Ah, beauty! and he brushed his hand over his hump.

Or else he ate a slice of jellied roast meat or bread and dripping. He left "his child" to cut the bread herself, "she was good at that." If her slice turned out too thick, he pushed it away, saying: Half of that would do! or: Try again! Then she would have to cut it again lengthwise, or at least try to. If he started to enjoy something, he cried: Enough, enough! and pushed it a long way away from him. Sometimes he cried: Amputando! and when she asked what that meant, he said: Clear it away and put it in the cupboard, because it's not going to tidy itself away! While she sat there with red earlobes, listening, he would tell her something. He said that "in our latitudes people forget to push their plates away. They eat three times as much as would be healthy for them!" Especially such people as "didn't earn their living from the sweat of their brows," but, like himself, merely sat surrounded by books, and shouldn't really eat at all.

But they must need something, said the Stechardess, otherwise they'll starve!

Only a little bit, said Lichtenberg, a very little bit! and he looked over at the corner where his work was waiting for him. He wanted to go on, on! but he didn't feel able to push the Stechardess into the other room, and close the door after her.

Make time fruitful, was something Lichtenberg often said at the time. Then he would take up his pen. He was forever "plunging into something," or "taking up the burden" or "dealing with something," even if it was just a little sentencelet. Which he would write down. He avoided his colleagues.

He owned a gilded grandfather clock, a gift from George III. A clockmaker visited him every week and wound it up for him so that "I know just when I've got stuck." He owned certain words that he loved and kept going back to, like "dulled" or "petrified" or "hard-bound" or "all felt out." (Himself at the beginning of his love.) Those words cropped up regularly with him, even when they were least appropriate. When he took a turn on the town walls, he would talk to himself. He talked about his "ideas that lay petrified on the bottom of his brain," (this in connection with the novel he meant to write at the time, and that Dietrich would publish. The hero was to be a crippled alchemist.)

In the evening, he strolled around the market with his wig on. The stalls were all empty. Lichtenberg had had a little snifter. He strolled through the same streets as everyone else. All of a sudden he was terribly bored. Then he would write something in his head, and think up new sentences for it. For example, sentences with which we describe someone who is drunk. He came up with:

> He can no longer lift his tongue.
> The way he walks, it's as though all the houses
>   belonged to him.
> He has had too much of a good thing.
> He is so full, he can feel it in his throat with his fingers.
> He is crookedly laden.

He mistakes a church tower for an overlarge toothpick.
He looks like a duck in a lightning storm.
He's as full as a set of bagpipes.
He takes a man in a red coat for a strawberry.
He sees two suns.
He has lately come from a good place, and so on.

Because he was able to come up with all that—and more, much more!—he hoped he was about to see or smell or think something extraordinary, something absolutely unprecedented, that he could write down in his notebook. He kept his finger ready in the place where he had got to. And so he went down the Weender Strasse, and then up it again. But no idea came to him, and he walked home.

He often petrified, and it was like this:

He got home, locked the door behind him, and said: I am not at home!

What about me, asked the Stechardess, laying her arm round his shoulders, are you not at home to me either?

And Lichtenberg said: No, nor for you either!

Then the Stechardess would cry a bit, and Lichtenberg would lie down in his bed. In the course of the following day, word of his condition would spread up and down the street. People called up to him a lot, and knocked on his door. But instead of calling out: Come on in! as he usually did, he cried: Get lost! I don't want to see anyone! In a word, he was mixed up, and he knew why as well. Göttingen, he thought, this tip of academe! This was where they had built it up, and now it languished there in boredom. How could he be expected to live here? He was reminded of Erxleben, who was through with it all, including the police, the polis, the pretty please, the pease porridge hot, the pease porridge cold, the petty pleasures . . .

At last the day came to an end. And the night?

People lit candles. Some they put in corners, others on tables. Now there was no more knocking on Lichtenberg's door, except in the event of someone dying.

Now that we're alone again, said Lichtenberg, things are looking up again! I hope you aren't scared of me, and that you've stopped crying!

She shook her head.

Good, he said, after all we have something to look forward to! You remember, don't you?

I think so, she said, blushing. Then she laughed again.

Lichtenberg took her hand and pressed it against his cheek. Then he took it off his cheek and pressed it against his heart. Maybe he would give it a kiss too. Let's creep back to where we lately emerged from with tired eyes, he said. And let's carry on from the place we got to, where we don't need candles or spectacles. Do you remember where that was?

I think so!

Exactly there, said Lichtenberg.

18.

ONCE, THE EVENING COACH from Hanover contained a gentleman who brought Lichtenberg a sealed letter. The letter smelled of lavender and sage, and it came from the King of England. He had a task for him which honored him, but also bewildered him. Lichtenberg would have to take his cane and his wig and go away for a long time. The task would sunder them, him and his little girl. The King had sent along a quadrant from England, the coachman was just bearing it into the house. The King desired Lichtenberg to measure the geographical longitude of His towns Hanover and Osnabrück. That was far from simple. Lichtenberg had the envoy who had brought the Royal letter step into the middle of his three rooms, and sent the Stechardess out. He was an elegant gentleman. Unfortunately, he was a little unmannerly, and kept looking at Lichtenberg's hunchback. He would have very much liked to touch it, only he didn't dare ask. That evening, Lichtenberg smiled a lot, and he listened to everything the envoy had to say. The army engineers were seeking reference points for an exact map of the Royal Duchy of Hanover and the Earldom of Osnabrück. These were to be supplied by Lichtenberg.

By me, Lichtenberg kept exclaiming.

Yes, sir!

As always when he was surprised, Lichtenberg had clammy hands. He rubbed them first on his trousers and then on his coat. "Every surprise," he wrote, "changes the world!" He ran up and down the room, and tweaked at his wig. Yes, it was still there! Then he saw to his consternation that the Stechardess had left some of her garments lying around, stockings and a pair of knickers. His noble visitor had seen them, and was avidly circling around them. When they were in front of him, he could hardly take his eyes off them, and he kept licking his lips. Lichtenberg would have liked to hide them, but that wasn't so easy. Everything in the room remained as it was until the end of the visit.

The following morning, following his constitutional in the garden, Lichtenberg had himself driven to Hanover at the Royal Exchequer's expense, to set the quadrant. He had got into new clothes, the accent this time on blue. Under his arm he had a velvet-lined box, which he pressed tightly to himself. Inside was a precision clock manufactured by the Göttingen clockmaker, Kampe. In his other hand, he held a telescope. With that, "to assure himself of his spuriousness," he kept peeking up at the sky, and counting the stars. Both telescope and clock were expensive items, he had saved up for them all his life. The quadrant had landed in his lap. Like all his many other bits of equipment, the Stechardess picked it up and polished it. Now you'll see it more easily, she said, putting it back in its place. When she wasn't in the room, he would go up to his equipment and kiss it. The Stechardess was an enthusiastic cleaner of his things, it was her way of contributing to his work. She also polished his clocks, saying: Now they'll run better. Lichtenberg kissed her on the mouth, and didn't disabuse her. Like other erroneous beliefs, this one brought them closer together.

Their last night together before his departure was a sad one. Because they had bolted the door, and put up thick winter curtains, they were able to hug and kiss freely. Then they took off each other's clothes. By God, they were both beautiful! They stretched out on the broad bed. He wanted to blow out the last candle, but then he let it burn. He wanted to see her for as long as he could. They were both thinking about their separation.

Do you know how many people live in big cities, asked Lichtenberg.

I bet it's a lot.

If you go for a walk in London, you will pass 3,666 in an hour.

Did you count them?

Yes. And all of them with different faces, purses and intentions, he said. Amazing that I ever found you!

And I you, she said.

So they crept together again. They kept looking at one another, so that they might remember the other. First she crept up on him, as she'd learned to do, and then he crept up on her. Of course, that was very nice. But he couldn't forget that tomorrow he'd be on the coach, and he didn't really concentrate.

Don't you love me any more, she asked.

Of course I do, he replied.

But not as much as before?

Of course I do, he replied.

When he had spilled himself into her, he hugged the child to himself for a while. She cried, first onto his face, and then over his shoulder. Then she fell asleep, while he remained awake for a long time.

The following morning, after sipping his coffee, he had himself helped into his blue coat by his girl. The weather was grey, appropriate for a parting. From time to time, a drop came out of the sky. Lots of people were standing in front of the house. They wanted to see tears. With his bare hands, Lichtenberg shoved away the onlookers, who liked to assemble every time somebody left. No standing around here! he said. He and his girl wanted to make use of their final minutes, they just didn't know how. A "crippling immobilism" had settled on them both.

You shouldn't have gone back inside the house again, she said.

Yes, I probably shouldn't!

Well then, go now!

She had quickly made herself beautiful for their leavetaking, so that she might be "as unforgettable as possible" in his memory. She had put on the newest of her dresses. She had got everything ready that he would need for his journey: the quadrant, the telescope, the maps, and a huge loaf of bread, because it had been another poor harvest, and there was no knowing whether there'd be anything in the shops in Hanover. The beggars were a scourge. They stood outside everyone's doors, including his own. On the bleaching-ground opposite, the goodwives had spread out the washing. The carriage that was to take him to Hanover and Osnabrück was already waiting, Lichtenberg couldn't delay it any longer. Word of his journey had got out. The neighbors were standing in their doorways, and were wearing dark waistcoats.

My child, said Lichtenberg, and drew the Stechardess to himself for the last time. What else could he say? He said: I'll return!

Yes, she said, I know you will!

I just need to go off for a while and do something with this equipment . . . He gestured at the boxes.

I know, she said. Then they kissed for the last time, and she went back into the house, where she would now be on her own. He had himself assisted into the carriage. Then he tossed a few coppers to the beggars, who came to blows over them. And with that the carriage trundled off.

For Lichtenberg, it was an important journey, one of the most important and saddest in his life. First, through steady rain, they made for Hanover. Well, that wasn't so far. There he slipped out of his cloak and took rooms in a little inn on the Speckstrasse. He had got Kampe to make him a magnetic needle, and he now went everywhere with that. He was wearing a purple wig, and he looked important. There were always people crowding around him, looking down at him. His method of measurement was novel. It depended on a precise observation of the lunar eclipse, an exact notation, using watch and telescope, of the satellites of Jupiter, and the obscuring of the stars by the moon.

In his thoughts, he was always with her.

Ever since I've had to leave her, I've felt more at home on the horizon than on the earth, he thought, and he pointed his telescope upwards. Since neither Hanover nor Osnabrück boasted an observatory, he instructed provisional observatories to be set up on the flatland. The changeable weather—winter descended overnight, and then went away just as suddenly—slowed his observing, his *stargazing*, as he called it in a letter. Because of the perennially overcast sky, he spent most of the time sitting in the inn, reduced instead to "the observing of women and girls." Nor was that straightforward, because they kept talking and never stood still. The King had sent him an assistant from London, someone by the name of Mr. Britain. He was his only companion. He had to clean his boots, polish up his equipment, and improve his English pronunciation. Lichtenberg would say: That's how you say it, isn't it? and Mr. Britain would reply: No, it's completely different!

But yesterday, said Lichtenberg, you assured me it was!

Perfectly possible, said Mr. Britain, yesterday it was different!

At night, he would run around after Lichtenberg, eyes fixed on the heavens, crying: Sir, I'm coming! If the sky was overcast, it meant the loss of a day. All that time, the Stechardess was sitting at home, pining for him, just as Lichtenberg was pining for her, although he was somewhere else. He sat with

Mr. Britain in their room at the inn, or he lay next to him on the big creaky inn bed, staring up at the ceiling. He lay on the right side of the bed, Mr. Britain on the left. Both had spread out their arms, and stretched their legs. The short, stout arms and legs of Lichtenberg, and the long, skinny ones of Mr. Britain. He always fell asleep first, while Lichtenberg lay awake for a long time. He had to think about his little Stechardess, and forgot all about the stars. Sometimes he tugged at Mr. Britain's sleeve for so long until he woke, and Lichtenberg could talk to him again. He was always talking about her.

Yes, sir, said Mr. Britain, when Lichtenberg had once again pulled him out of his sleep, what is it now?

Not much, said Lichtenberg, I just thought of something that I wanted to ask you about!

Me, sir, asked Mr. Britain.

Yes, you, said Lichtenberg. I wanted to ask you if you had a wife.

No, sir, said Mr. Britain, no wife!

Or a mistress?

Nor that either!

Why not, asked Lichtenberg. Don't you like women?

I like them all right, said Mr. Britain, but from a distance!

Whereas I like them from close up, said Lichtenberg, there are some who can't be close enough for me! Yes, not close enough! Then he would be quiet again. Someone walked up the steps and disappeared into his room. Was it just one, or was it possibly a couple? Then Lichtenberg started talking some more, whereas Mr. Britain would have preferred to sleep. What is it, cried Lichtenberg, why aren't you saying anything any more? Why don't you ask me any questions?

What shall I ask you?

Ask me if I have a wife.

You?

Yes, me! Ask away! If I feel like telling you, I'll tell you!

The young Englishman lay there in their shared bed, in his white vest and his white pants, and sometimes he bumped into him with his feet. He had his hands folded behind his head. It would never have occurred to him that the little man might have a wife.

Well, asked Lichtenberg, what would you like to know about me?

I'd like to know if you've got a wife, asked the young Englishman, and he yawned.

Yes, I do, said Lichtenberg, I do! Then there was another pause. Well, he asked, isn't there anything else you want to know? Why are you such a sluggardly conversationalist? Come on!

I'd like to know if you're married to her, asked the Englishman, and Lichtenberg replied: Not yet! We're taking our time!

Are you indeed, said Mr. Britain, and Lichtenberg asked: What about you? What's your opinion of marriage? Or don't you ever want to get married? but by then the young Englishman had dropped off again. Nothing brings as much equanimity to a conversation as not having an opinion, thought Lichtenberg. Then he crept out of his side of the bed to write it down: "Nothing brings as much equanimity to a conversation . . ." He crept back in with Mr. Britain, propped himself up for a while and looked out onto the street. He preferred to look up at the sky, and hoped for that "miraculous heavenly body," the moon. If you think about it for long enough, it's bound to come, he thought.

When they had observed the Hanoverian heavens for long enough, they packed everything up again, and got into their carriage. Now they were headed for Osnabrück! Since the bad weather persisted, and there seemed little prospect of any improvement, they put on their thick trousers and looked about the countryside. Lichtenberg being so small, he liked to look up, for the view, as he said. He preferred to have the countryside below him. Sometimes he asked Mr. Britain to lift him onto a wall. There, he thought of girls again.

Are you going to marry her then, your sweetheart, Lichtenberg asked.

I don't have a sweetheart.

But I do, said Lichtenberg contentedly. When we're back, I'm going to ask her if she'll have me.

You, sir?

Why not, asked Lichtenberg.

Once, when the moon had gone hiding, and looked certain not to reappear in a hurry, they made a detour to Hamburg, at the King's expense. Mr. Britain bundled Lichtenberg into a big open cart and climbed in after him. The cart, as ever, was full. They trundled along. To pass the time, there was a lot of talking. Some, of course, merely nodded. So that no one would see his titchy legs, Lichtenberg had gotten a woollen blanket from the coachman, and spread it over his knees.

Thank you, he said, that's much better!

Then he softly closed his eyes, and let whatever it might be pass in review: forests, lakes, flat land, small animals, the occasional human. This is, he thought, the wrong landscape for me, I would much rather be in Göttingen! He longed for Göttingen, where lampposts stood on the street corners, and the Stechardess peeped out from behind every reasonable sized tree. When he had been silent for long enough, he began to talk. At first, he talked about ancient Professor Wollmann, his colleague, who was forever getting lost, and once suddenly turned up in his, Lichtenberg's, lecture room. Wollmann, said Lichtenberg, hangs around the university like a beautiful old candelabrum that hasn't shed any light for twenty years!

Why no light, asked a fellow traveller, and Lichtenberg replied: He's burnt out!

When a fat man climbed in to join them, and jammed everyone else into corners, Lichtenberg said out loud: There are people who are so fat they can laugh under cover of their own lard! Then he laughed himself, so loud that it was audible in the forests. The others laughed with him. The fat man clenched his fist and grunted. Then he fell asleep.

And when, asked Lichtenberg, is this Hamburg place going to come? and Mr. Britain said: If only one knew!

When it rained, they huddled closer together in their coach, and let the drops run down them. Their conversation slowed and finally dried up entirely. They watched the drips. A few of those beside him started to cough, with others it took the form of sneezing. At the next inn, all cried out: Thank God! and life returned to them. One dried himself off and moaned, another was looking for a handkerchief, a third chewed chest pastilles and said: They won't help either! That was already in Hamburg, where they settled into a cheap inn. The next morning, they looked out of the inn windows and saw the beggar boys and the dogs. They sniffed the fresh sea air and cried: It smells of the wide world! Some boys were given coins by Lichtenberg, but not all of them of course. How could he, with his little money, provide for the whole world? At noon, they promenaded arm in arm along the Alster. All the impressions that swarmed in upon them there!

The wide skirts of all the fancy ladies and the elevation of their coiffures, the overlong dresses that trailed along the ground, they took it all in. They drank ale, ate mussels and sea-fish, and looked at the girls with less than burning interest, seeing as one of them was provided for and the other wasn't that way inclined. Because Mr. Britain walked so fast, Lichtenberg had to keep stopping to shake his head. Not one of the many girls they saw was right for him. The right one was sitting by the window in Göttingen, and probably staring her eyes out, looking for him. With his cripple's vanity, he stalked swiftly past the girls after lunch. At night he slept better, on account of the fresh salt air that he hadn't sniffed since his last visit to England. Sometimes, if he was in luck, he dreamed of his beautiful child. Another time he dreamed he was travelling and had booked into an inn, where there wasn't just eating and drinking, but also dicing. Opposite him was a windy fellow who was just eating his soup, and not paying any attention to what was going on around him. But how peculiar: every second or third spoonful, he chucked up into the air. Then he caught the soup on his spoon and drank it. (Lichtenberg would have this dream once more, shortly before his death.) Or else he dreamed his bed was too hard. Somebody must have stolen the feathers, and replaced them with gravel. Because birds with feathers like that simply couldn't be! When he had got a leg out of bed in the morning, he felt a little better. Then he would grab hold of Mr. Britain, and pull the other one out after. Sometimes Mr. Britain would tuck him in at night, but then the bed weighed on him to such an extent that "his legs fell asleep before the rest of him, and it took him a long time to sleep up with them." The following day, the pair of them slipped into their jackets, put on their wigs, and headed out. They wanted to see fresh sights.

Fresh sights, always fresh sights, cried Lichtenberg. He had carved himself a stick. And so he marched into Hamburg. From time to time he stopped to exclaim: Well, I never! Then he wrote something down in his notebook, or swished his stick through the air. Or else he exclaimed: I'm not having that! and he would again swish his stick. Sometimes he hoped to hit a fly, but he never managed. Of course, he really wanted to do something else, namely to return to Göttingen. He was just wandering around to while away the time till the next full moon. In the inn, they drank their beer from large tankards, because that made the fish taste better. He ate the little bones too, because they were so nice and crispy.

I can see you choking on those one day, said Mr. Britain.

Bah, stuff, said Lichtenberg. Fishbones are healthy!

They looked at the Hamburg houses and the people who were in the world with them, and who stood around beside them. In Göttingen he would remember them. Sometimes he would shout: Hang on! and Mr. Britain would stop. Then they spoke about what they happened to see just then, above and below. Man, said Lichtenberg, has been put into the world to deal with the surface of the earth. Everything higher or lower is the preserve of Nature herself.

And what is higher or lower, asked Mr. Britain, and Lichtenberg said: Quite so, absolutely!

They inspected the house of the chief pastor Goeze, who wanted to have people dragged into heaven by the hair. But they would sooner have their hair pulled out than listen to him, that's the way they are, Lichtenberg said. Wonder if he's dragged many people there yet, he asked, but Mr. Britain didn't understand, and they trotted on. Mr. Britain was wearing his blue waistcoat, Lichtenberg his green one. He often stopped. His waistcoat and his jacket rapidly tightened on him with the good food and the good beer, and Lichtenberg tugged at them. It was time to go home, each to their respective home. The last morning, they were propped on the windowsill again, side by side. They surveyed the piece of street the landlord had offered them.

How do you mean: offered, asked Mr. Britain.

Allocated, said Lichtenberg in English, for three days! Now there's just half of one left!

They put their wigs on for the last time, one wig was human hair, the other was hemp, and for the last time they trotted through the city. Since the whole city was too much for them, they at least trotted through half of it. As they did so, they imitated the people they passed, and then the frogs and quails. Finally the milk- and radish-maids, whom they larked about with. When they saw one who was especially pretty, Mr. Britain pinched her cheeks and called her "my beauty." Then he took out his handkerchief, said: Faugh! and wiped his hand clean. Lichtenberg was now certain that Mr. Britain didn't really like girls. For his part, he would happily have groped them, but they were a little high for him. Besides, he kept having to think of that other who was sitting at home, and was surely looking out for him. The next morning, the two men would part. Already, they weren't talking to each other much. Then they would pile into their respective coaches and go home.

19.

*I*T WAS, WITH SUN AND WIND and rain, their first summer of love. They were inseparable. They smiled a lot. In sleep, they reached their arms out to one another, and looked for each other. And found each other too. Then they kissed each other pitilessly and fell asleep again. Later, they turned to lie on their sides, he a little further down. When one wanted to turn round, he said: Come with me, darling! and took the other with him. When they woke up, they wished each other a good morning, and asked one another if they'd slept well, and what dreams they'd had. The Stechardess had to be quick to tell hers, because she forgot them quickly. Lichtenberg dreamed slowly and scientifically, and that was more durable. He took his dream along into his day, but by the time he was ready to write it down, it generally wasn't useful.

He always wanted to have her around him. Often he went to get her.

Or don't you want, he asked, and she said: If you want, then so do I! and he said: Good girl! or: All right then!

Now it was the turn of love again, he was the first to creep into bed. He took off his wig, so as not to crush it. Then he hugged his girl and undressed her and kissed her on the mouth and the breasts and the thighs. How often now he had kissed and undressed and "jumped on" her, as he said (and wrote). (He left her to dress herself.) When undressing he was impatient, and said: Hurry up, little slow coach! He had lots of pet names for her, they seemed to collect: my rascal girl, my sun star, lucky charmer, etcetera. When they were lying in bed—"our bed is always a heavenly bed" *—and a student or colleague was standing downstairs knocking at the door, he laid his finger across her mouth and said: Let him yell! Or he sighed, got up and said: Just a minute! Then he put his coat back on, went out, and shut the bedroom door behind him. To the visitor, invariably a man, he said: Oh, you again!

Am I bothering you?

To tell you the truth: I really don't want to see anyone, said Lichtenberg. But if you must! He let him in and pushed him into the corner with the vacuum pump. Don't touch it! he said. Where, he asked, had we got to?

They sat close together, and Lichtenberg was forced to listen. It took a while. Next door, his girl was lying in the big bed, alone and warm. The visitor had leaned against the wall and was talking and talking. Till Lichtenberg suddenly leaped up and called: Well, that's it then! and the visitor stood up as well and said: Yes, I suppose it is! Then Lichtenberg dragged him to the front door and pushed him outside. He slammed the door shut, and bolted it. Then he shouted: I gave him the bum's rush! Now I'm on my way back to you!

Afterwards they lay side by side again, breathing deeply. If he wanted to please her, he asked: Do you know what you are now? She shook her head and said no. Then he said: You're my wife now! She went red and sighed. Then she shook her

*The German word for "fourposter bed" is *Himmelbett*, literally a "heavenly bed."

head again—her "naughty little head"—and said: But we're not married! and he said: Oh yes we are. We will be! Maybe! He wanted, without going too far, to tie her to himself as tightly and securely as he could. Then he put his hand to his forehead, and said: Or what shall I do? In reality, he shrank back from the thought.

Sometimes, after they had been lying side by side like that for a long time, he felt changed. He went to the mirror and thought he had become more upright. He almost asked the Stechardess what she thought, but in the end he didn't. She would have told me if she'd noticed something different about me, he thought. Everything takes time!

The next summer too—their third—also boasted lofty skies, clear and cloudless. That was how Lichtenberg saw them anyway, and how he described them in his wastebook. He was sporting a white shirt and a dark waistcoat. His collar was dashingly open. Lichtenberg had climbed onto his thick Latin dictionary and was looking out of the open window. He often talked to himself, in Latin, he said to the Stechardess, so that you don't know what I think of you!

Ever since his colleagues learned that he had some "young creature to talk to him in Latin and sleep with him in French," they stopped going to see him. They trotted past his door, and "didn't want to bother him." They're lying around up there, and even after three years it seems they can't get enough of one another, they said and pointed up at the window. There, they said, is where he's put her!

Yes, said another, she's forever sitting around with him!

If they're not actually lying around, you mean, said another.

Yes, said the first, I expect she needs a lie-down from time to time!

In that marvellous time, Lichtenberg was not free from worries. One had to do with his health. When the Stechardess asked him about it quietly, he asked: What health? Or, ironically: I have looked into the register of illnesses and seen that I have a full set! He had eaten—broth and potatoes. He was wheezing slightly. There is as little to be said of my health, he said, as there is about my death! As long as it hasn't arrived . . . And if it has . . . That point, he said, has been dealt with! No further bulletins! Thus passes . . . Well, what do you think? Right, he said, life too!

When he had spent long enough sitting at the window with her once, he went out, *alone*. He was all gussied up, in color, with gold and silver, and fools' gold and fools' silver, as he put it. As he stood in the doorway, looking uneasily up at the sky, the Stechardess asked him: Are you looking for something? and Lichtenberg said: Yes, the sun.

Sometimes he walked as far as the old paper mill, talking to himself in English or Latin. Sometimes he walked down the Untere Klarspule and the Kornstrasse, and looked at the crumbling houses.

Sometimes he looked for something else, for instance . . . Erxleben was of course long-buried, and was in the process of dissolution. Previously they had often come here on their walks together, one on the left, the other on the right. Because Erxleben walked faster, Lichtenberg had often had to grab hold of his sleeve, and call: Not so fast! He could remember that well. When he tried to remember other details from their friendship, he often came up without anything. He knew something had to have been, but he could no longer remember what. When he mentioned Erxleben to the Stechardess—often he didn't even mean to, he just slipped out—it was in rather general terms. It was all he could think of. Sometimes, without telling her, he went along to Erxleben's tomb. On the way, he might pluck a narcissus or a primrose or two, and lay them on it. When he returned, he would tell the Stechardess about it, and she would ask, as ever: And then?

He always used to stand there, said Lichtenberg, pointing from the window at a certain—uncertain—point.

And what did he do there, asked the Stechardess.

Cough, he said.

Dr. Blumenbach lived three houses away. He was working on a treatise on the "Love of Animals," which, according to him, was faithful and strong. Lichtenberg was telling her about a love like that, and showing her how great it was. Then he had to kiss her again, because she was so overcome. After that they talked about the murderer Ruttgerodt, who had recently been hanged by his short neck in Göttingen. Lichtenberg had wanted to go and watch, but had ended up staying home on her account. Instead, he had trotted along to the university the following day, and had been told all about it. The Stechardess couldn't understand murderers, she just shook her head.

In order truly to understand a person, you have to be that person, Lichtenberg claimed.

You mean, you would understand him then? All right then, does a person understand himself?

Possibly.

They had now divided the days—and the times of the day—into various activities. Everything now followed a more orderly rhythm. Sometimes it was time for the milk, sometimes for the bread, and sometimes for the laundrywoman. The Stechardess brought the laundry to the front door, and then she returned to her kitchen. We thank you! she said, or: Till the next time! Those who didn't know her took her for his child, but "out of wedlock." The little Stechardess ran all over his apartment, clearing everything up, from his cravat to his boots. For the cravat, she had a brush, for the shoes a soft cloth. The cloth was kept in the little kitchen, and was often produced. Just a minute! she would say, and when he asked: Why? she said: I'm going to perform a little operation on you! and she cleaned his shoes.

Sometimes a letter would arrive for him, the Stechardess waved it around in the air. Then it was chop-chop straight into the study. In her curiosity, the Stechardess followed in his wake. The door slammed shut behind them, and they read the letter together. Hufeland announced an impending visit, his bags were already packed, Gleim had composed a new poem, he enclosed a few sample lines from it. The Stechardess could now read all the words, but she often didn't understand what they meant together. Sometimes she read aloud to him, and he would explain to her what she had read. He drew up little lists, which she put in a desk drawer. They were lists of books, names and places, of students who would come to see him. Or else they were "Lists of illnesses about which I have thought too much, and from which I am now suffering."

Are you really suffering from them, or are you just saying that, asked the Stechardess.

I am suffering.

Tell me some of them, just for example, she asked, but Lichtenberg shook his head and merely repeated: I am suffering!

"Here is," he wrote on a piece of paper, "this summer!"

What do you mean by that?

That that will have been this summer, he replied.

Lichtenberg was wearing the green waistcoat. Makes a change, he thought. When it got still warmer, he took it off as well. He stepped up to the mirror and said to himself: It seems to me I am going through some change again! I think this is what they refer to as *quiet happiness*! He was wearing his yellow—"his youthful"—wig, and was chasing the Stechardess through the garden. When he was out of puff, she would stop as well and ask: Aren't you coming?

Yes, yes, he said, I'm coming. I just had a thought!

You're out of breath, aren't you, she asked, and Lichtenberg said: No, no, I'm fine! and he pressed his hand down on his heart.

Sometimes she took pity on him, and allowed him to catch her.

It was summer again—or it was still summer. Every nook smelled of something different, but they all smelled good. They ran round a tree, then along the fence. When Lichtenberg really couldn't manage any more, he sat down and said: Now pay attention! Then, rather fulsomely, he explained to her all about the steam engine. There were children in front of the house, who wanted to get a sight of his hunchback. They stuck their noses through the fence and peeped through the gaps. Would he catch the girl? Then she was lying in his arms again, and they were kissing each other. The Stechardess had to kiss downwards, Lichtenberg upwards. Was anyone watching them? He dragged her off into the lilac corner. It wasn't blooming any more, but it surely would again. At any rate, Lichtenberg pulled her down on top of him and up against him and said: There's something I have to tell you! He panted, and he pulled her very close. You won't believe what I have to tell you, he said.

I'll believe anything you tell me, said the child.

You won't believe it, he said, but I feel as if my hunchback was gone!

What hunchback, she asked.

20.

*A*T THE END OF APRIL, the snow disappeared as quickly as it had arrived. "Always these changing seasons," Lichtenberg wrote in his diary. "So now it's raining again!" Then a coach drew up in front of the house on the Gotmarstrasse, and a Hungarian gentleman climbed out of it. He was dressed, like all Hungarians, in a red coat with gold buttons. He was tall, fair and freckled, and didn't look at all Hungarian. If you asked him a question in German, he wouldn't understand it all. If you asked him how he was getting on, he would say: Ichabod! or: More or less! When Lichtenberg asked him, he said: I'm alive! But that's neither here nor there! Then Lichtenberg closed the door behind him, and the man from Hungary was standing in his drawing room. He had leapt out of his carriage into the rain, and had gotten rather wet. Now he was dripping hugely. Lichtenberg had turned pink, as he always did when he had an unexpected visitor. He pushed the Stechardess, he had just been playing with her a bit—into the kitchen. Then he confronted the Hungarian.

Do we have any mutual friends, asked Lichtenberg. Gleim! Reimarus! Who else?

Since Lichtenberg's Hungarian was not good, he said a couple of sentences in English. The Hungarian, his name was Dr. Imredy, made an apologetic gesture, and carried on in French. Lichtenberg said: Comme vous preferez! and looked at him in the rainy dark as closely as he could. First he viewed him from one side, then from the other. Concerning the head, to which he was now looking up, he had heard many good things. For the moment, however, it was dripping. Lichtenberg said: Pardon! ran to the linen cupboard, and fetched a towel for him. He studied his sorry, rain-afflicted wig of human hair, and shook his head. God knows what type of skull and what type of thoughts might be under there! He saw that the Hungarian was a great scholar from a humble background, and he asked him not to be ashamed, but to slip out of his coat, and hang it up to dry in front of the fire. This Dr. Imredy did. He was wearing a grey camisole which he would certainly have filled, if only his wife had given him more to eat. Unfortunately, there wasn't any more. When he had said thank you and rubbed himself dry for a sufficient time, he returned the wet towel to Lichtenberg. He said: Un petit moment! and he scouted round the corner where the Stechardess had vanished. She was of great interest to the Hungarian. She came out, curtseyed, and took receipt of the wet towel.

Your daughter, asked Dr. Imredy.

No, said Lichtenberg in his peculiar French, the girl is employed by me in various capacities in my large house and garden. She is a very handy person to have around, he said, and the Stechardess smiled and disappeared again. The Hungarian hungrily watched her go, and kept looking in the direction of the kitchen door. He said: Une jolie fille!

Decidement, said Lichtenberg, and then, to turn his thoughts to other matters: The door of my study, and most particularly the key to the door, stinks of printer's ink, because I am a writer. Can you smell it? It's revolting, isn't it, he asked, and Dr. Imredy said again: Decidement!

Outside, it was still raining. They had sat down. They were now speaking about a mutual acquaintance, who was based, like the Hungarian, in Leiden, and had come forward with a thesis on the responsiveness of certain ganglia.

In frogs, asked Lichtenberg.

No, said Imredy, in people!

Isn't he still a little young to be doing that, asked Lichtenberg. I know the man. I once pissed in the same chamberpot as him, I remember the occasion well! But nowadays babes and infants like to have their way with the sciences, and as the scientific organ is still incapable of standing, these cases rarely pass off without a great deal of rubbing. But I take it he's still alive, or not, he asked, and the Hungarian said: Oh yes, oh yes!

In that case, said Lichtenberg, will you ask him to write to me of his contemporary appearance, about the face and hair in particular, so that I can form a picture of him for myself. He has children, doesn't he? Ask him how many for me, and whether male or female. Ask him if it's true that when a man becomes a father, he has to buy a large wig, a flowered dressing gown and yellow slippers, and from time to time to stand by the window with his long pipe in his mouth, and the tobacco tamper on his little finger, so that all may see him.

Very well, said Professor Imredy, I'll ask him!

Both of them now had long pipes jammed in their mouths, so the conversation could now begin in earnest. Professor Imredy was no longer dripping so badly, he was getting dryer. Only the coachman was still dripping, because he was standing in the rain, but that didn't really matter because he was in his coachman's greatcoat and he belonged to the staff. When a drop fell off the Hungarian and landed on the floor, he quickly trod on it so that no one would notice. As always, when someone was visiting him for the first time, Lichtenberg was preoccupied with his picayune stature, and was rather excitable. He made mistakes with his French. He talked about the punch slopping around in the kettle that "the little girl" was brewing.

Une jolie fille, the Hungarian kept repeating. What's her name, he asked, and Lichtenberg smiled and said: Mademoiselle Stechard from the Wendenstrasse in Göttingen, the daughter of decent but impoverished parents. He wanted the punch served piping hot, it wasn't hot enough yet. Lichtenberg, in his yellow wig, kept making mistakes, and said "peeping hot" for "piping hot." That was caused by the excitement of having a visitor. He repeated the words "peeping hot" a few times more, but they were still wrong. Then in came the Stechardess with the punch, which really was hot now. Le voila, le punch, cried Lichtenberg, and the Stechardess set it down on the table.

When darkness had fallen over the rain-bound town of Göttingen, and the two scholars were taking their punch in small sips, the conversation began to perk up. More was said. They discussed the weather, first in Hungary, then in Göttingen. In Hungary, it tended to be dry, in Göttingen damp. Though, then again, it could sometimes be damp in Hungary and dry in Göttingen. On this occasion, however . . . What a year for storms, so much was coming down, quite unasked for! Sometimes, like an old woman, Lichtenberg tied a cloth round his head, over his wig. Then he took a deep breath and "charged into the Göttingen storm." I leap, he said, into a carriage, and have myself driven around in the rain, or perhaps under the rain, first this way, then that. That's my secret, that's where I get my best ideas from! Ideas are, as I like to say, the backdrop of the world, everything takes place in front of a prospect of ideas. But like a good salad, they need to be mixed and tossed. And my word for that is . . . well, what was it again?

Well?

Rhetoric, said Lichtenberg in French. When he sat in the carriage in winter, with his wig on his head, and his ideas inside it, then he would get *all snuggled up*. Whatever that is in French! His foot-muff—or that?!—reached up to his oxters. And then he'd be lovely and warm. He would get a bit of fresh air, though, admittedly, not much exercise.

Very interesting, said his Hungarian visitor. And what else do you get up to?

The first thing Lichtenberg looked for in life—the "adorable child" was sitting just beside him—was a fine, warm, quiet place from which to make his observations. He observed the dead world and the living. Of living creatures, he observed both the upper and the lower, and of the upper, well . . . He observed men and women, horses, young dogs, cats, he made no distinctions. Then he took another deep breath, because his heart was thumping so. He had them approach him, the women in their long skirts, their narrow waists and their high heels that one could hear tapping away at a distance. Now, he thought to himself, open your eyes, something is heading your way! Such days were always wonderful.

The girls wore bonnets, that's what they approached him in. Underneath were their round heads, which he liked to stroke, sometimes, if necessary, even for money.

Vous dites, exclaimed Dr. Imredy in astonishment.

Then, like my friend Lavater, I claim to be a phrenologist, said Lichtenberg, and for them it's part of their job. I take great delight in that. It always happens, he said, like this. Lichtenberg, who would so much have liked to be taller and handsomer and broader and straighter, looked at the girls with staring eyes. He didn't look them in the eyes, he didn't dare to do that. He pretended to be looking past them. That was a trick, though. Looking at them was the only pleasure he then—he looked at the Stechardess—had. There they were, walking up to him in their high heels, and with their silky walks. Usually it was a Sunday, or it would shortly be Sunday. They were coming from church or going to church, and they were pretty to look at. The girls were talking to each other, and Lichtenberg, who so often was hard of hearing, understood every word. We're having beans today, said one, what about you? or: Look, there's a cute fellow, he has strong calves! And so they passed Lichtenberg, whom they never referred to. They had some bit of stone or metal tied round their wrists. Lichtenberg didn't have strong calves, and he wore no metal on his wrist. He was generally a solitary figure on the street, and the girls felt sorry for him. The friends of his younger days asked him what he did with himself, and he said: Top secret! or: I'll tell you when I'm dead! Forster, who just then happened to be back in Göttingen, wrote: "I hardly see anything of him, because one rarely meets this eccentric, who withdraws from all human society, at a propitious moment, and the sight of his awkward expression makes me awkward, as I stand on his doorstep." At that time, he told Dr. Imredy, I lived largely on, well, can you guess?

On sentences?

Not a bit of it, on medicaments! It was the two Göttingen pharmacists, Renner and Klein, who kept him going. Last winter, they had each taken more than thirty talers off him. To look at him walking through Göttingen, you would have thought: he's not worth that much! He was incapable of going past either establishment without popping inside and describing his symptoms to the man behind the counter. Who always had a suitable remedy too. When Lichtenberg emerged from the shop, he would have it in his hand. In his right, he would carry the tinctures he needed, and in his left the powders, and at night he rubbed himself down with the embrocations he stuffed in his coat pocket. The minute he was home, he flung himself upon his purchases. "I only need to walk past a pharmacy to lose half a pound of coppers," he wrote to Gleim. All Göttingen knew by now what the little fellow was steeped in from top to bottom. For breakfast, he drank star anise tea, "a proper pailful." Against the toothache, he poured a mixture of brandy and warm water into his mouth in the morning. Then he gargled with that for a couple of hours. Instead of spitting it out afterwards, he said: All right, I'll sacrifice myself! and he bravely gulped it all down. In the afternoon, it was fresh air. He wrapped woollen cloths round his legs and went for a walk. And in the evening, so that Morpheus would come, he drank a pail of double beer. Then he cried: I can't go on like this any longer! and wanted to enjoy life more. On one afternoon, he smoked six pipes of Dutch tobacco, and drank four bottles of English ale. He felt dizzy, and went up to the window and asked himself why. He looked out. Unfortunately no one was coming up the street just then, to help him with his reeling. So he shut the window again, and buried his nose in a book. "These days," he wrote to Blumenbach, who by now had fifty-nine skulls cluttering up his windowsills, "a dilettante is better off than we scientific day-laborers. We are incapable of keeping anything in order. My electrical equipment needs a room to itself, which I am unable to provide. I boil and bake in my room, I receive students there, and each time I assay a little experiment, there are a hundred others sweating over it with me. I have to reckon on two hundred boots on my floorboards, a thousand sweating toes."

Et alors, asked the Hungarian visitor.

Well, said Lichtenberg, well!

The Hungarian had yet to say what the purpose of his visit was. In truth, he was a distraction. It was a post day, and Lichtenberg didn't want to miss it. He thought of all the people to whom he ought to write long letters. Then he would scuttle across to his desk and . . . Once, in fog, a servant had ridden full tilt into the axle of a post chaise, so that his poor animal was impaled on the pole, or should it be impoled. Lichtenberg, who was about to lecture on Deluc's theory of pain, saw and heard everything. He ran into his bedroom, flung himself onto his bed, and didn't eat for two days. Nor was he able to read and write anything either. It was a while ago now. The horse had long since been devoured by rats and poor people. Lichtenberg still saw it when he closed his eyes. Kästner advised him to put his hand in front of his eyes and to stop thinking about it, but to use his reason and . . . "If I should use my reason," wrote Lichtenberg on a piece of paper, "it would be like someone who had always used his right hand, suddenly having to use his left." And then he put the piece of paper away again.

Et alors, said Dr. Imredy.

I go to the post a little later, said Lichtenberg.

On the day that Dr. Imredy sat damply in his apartment, wanting to say something—just what it was, everyone would hear before long—many other subjects were discussed first, for instance their favorite foods, and sensuality. The Stechardess was in the kitchen, frittering and boiling away. Lichtenberg had his wig on. He put a hand over his belly and said: Here it is! Then he reflected briefly, and cried: Tongue of veal! and Dr. Imredy said: Aha! Lichtenberg drank another glass, and described to his guest how it would melt in the mouth. He sat on his very highest chair, and looked down at the Hungarian. He was absolutely stuck on the tongue now. If, he said, you stirred the white wine sauce, and placed one's own, uncooked tongue squarely below the one that had been cooked, then . . . Finally the Stechardess came back. She moved up close to him, and put her small childlike hand on his hunchback. She said: Rice pudding with raisins! and Dr. Imredy, who, along with his many other languages, also understood a little German, said: Pudding is for children! He wanted something with paprika. That's the greatest gourmet delight I know! To date anyway, he said, but maybe I'm in for something still more delicious!

Oh God, said Lichtenberg, and looked at his girl. What a long time they had been together already! And it wasn't over yet, there was still this and that to come. Lichtenberg stood up. He pulled on a thicker coat, and defended the hygrometer. The Stechardess nodded and watched him. Then he showed off a bit, and claimed he had a hundred and thirty students. Finally he talked about the breaking up of water, which could be done by means of electrical sparks. The idea had also been taken up abroad, though they hadn't made much headway with it there. At any rate, it seemed not to be particularly easy to break up water. Well, maybe later, said Lichtenberg, who proposed to devote the next few days to his essay, "The Air-Bath." He was pro, by the way.

They talked a little more, and Lichtenberg thought: What does he want with me? The Stechardess was at her frittering. She had put a large piece of beef to roast on the fire. This she now served. Lichtenberg reached for the sharp knife, and cut the meat into thin slivers which were nice and pink. They were served with white bread and mild mustard and, for anyone who wanted, red wine. Of course, everyone did want. And there was a lot of talking. The Stechardess talked about a dress that Lichtenberg had given her, and the Hungarian talked about how pleased he was when he saw someone browsing in a book, and he noticed it was one of his. Lichtenberg confessed that he liked following girls up steps, especially steep steps. He could watch how their skirts tautened and then relaxed again. He couldn't see what was underneath, but he could imagine it.

You old roué, said the Hungarian, suddenly using the intimate form. Lichtenberg used it back to him. Then the Hungarian pointed at the Stechardess, and asked: Haven't you got her, and isn't she enough for you?

If you are patient enough, said Lichtenberg, in time everything will come to you, as if it had been a part of you all along.

Nothing comes, said Dr. Imredy, you have to claim it for yourself! And Lichtenberg put his arm round the shoulders of the Stechardess, and repeated: A part of me! He carved some more meat. Then he helped himself to another slice. The Hungarian couldn't say no, whereas the Stechardess . . .

By the way, said Dr. Imredy, who had had a lot to drink already, by the way! He hadn't come on his own account, he was an ambassador. The University of Leiden had sent him to knock on Lichtenberg's door. (At this point, he knocked on the wall.) How would he fancy becoming a professor in Holland? In Leiden, they had a pretty house all ready for him with a flower garden, and lots of people were waiting for him. There was a sizeable stipend and . . .

No, not Leiden, said Lichtenberg abruptly, and Imredy nodded and said: Well then!

They went on to talk about this and that, but in effect their conversation was over. Lichtenberg didn't want to go. He dreaded the long move and he "didn't want his only girl to stray around in foreign parts." He wanted her at home, "where no one could get at her and lay his hand on her shoulder, or anywhere south of there, for that matter." Because the idea, that merely with her eyes, she could bring a man to improper thoughts . . .

I understand, said the Hungarian, let's not talk about it any more, let's talk about the thing next door!

Outside, it had stopped raining. It was only dripping from the eaves.

Lichtenberg was tired. Likewise Dr. Imredy. He asked where he would sleep, and wanted to see his bed. It was a long way from her room, tucked away in a different wing of the apartment, with "large tracts full of science" separating the visitor and the Stechardess. Ah yes, he sighed. He asked Lichtenberg where they slept, she and Lichtenberg, and wanted to inspect "their beautiful resting-place," but Lichtenberg, though drunk, was obstinate, and refused to show it to him. He gestured perfunctorily in the direction where it apparently was, and said: There! Well, he cried, are you coming or not? and they went their separate ways. It wouldn't surprise me, said Lichtenberg, once he was finally alone with the "apple of his eye," if he groped for you in his sleep with his hands and his heart, but he won't find you. You're closely guarded when you're with me, he said, and he started yawning. Then the dwarf pulled off her corset and her chemise, and started to kiss her little titties. She wanted to say: Oh, you libertine! but all she said was: Oh you! By the time she was finally at his side, he was already asleep.

21.

EOPLE AS FAR AWAY AS Osnabrück now knew "what went on" in Lichtenberg's quiet house. They just expressed it in different ways. They talked about how he and the girl "were doing it together" or "shared beddy-byes," "went snogging and licking each other," that "they ate out of each other's hands," etc. At the university, everyone stared at him. The looks he got! When he had gone past with his stack of books, they shook their heads. Then they winked at each other and sucked their teeth: tsk tsk tsk! There wasn't much left of the sympathy he had once enjoyed as a cripple. The men were envious of him and asked: Wonder how he managed to catch her? or: Did he make her climb up on his hump, the little chit! He's got to have something!

Yes, said someone else, and I know where he keeps it too!

If you're talking about what he's got between his legs, well I've got one of those as well!

Me too, said a third.

Often Lichtenberg, just as at the very beginning, sat with her over his books, crying: On, on! A few were opened. Others had little slips of paper in them. That's how far I have to get today, he said to her. Other books lay on the sofa or the floor. The Stechardess pointed at one and said: Are you reading that one today?

Yes, that one!

But you read the other one yesterday.

True, he said, but today I'm reading this one!

To keep him from having to keep getting up, she fetched him what he needed, a bit of paper, some notes, a book. Then he would read it, or else look out of the window, which was often left open. Then along came the students, the dusk, the night. Because they were so happy, the days passed quickly. Only sometimes she said: I thought it was later than this! or: Wonder why time seems to have stood still today! Sometimes they played cards together, but often they were unsuccessful. Now they couldn't find a card, or they needed a third to play. It's too bad, he said, that two can't play! and he put the cards away again. He laid his hand on her little head, and thought: Everything is in there: her desires, her wishes, her fears! Yes, he thought, it's true! and he stroked her hair. Is your little man allowed to do this, he asked, as he pulled her corset and chemise over her head.

I feel shy, she said.

You what?

I ought to feel shy!

At dusk, he looked for lucifers or a taper, and if he couldn't find them, he called for her.

Wait, she said, and helped him look. The flame flickered in her face and "gave her a new one." He said: Come here, my love! and she climbed on top of him, or he on top of her.

Well, he said when it was over, was that lovely or what?

Yes, she said, it was lovely!

Or he laid his hand on her knee and she read to him by candlelight. Her reading was still a little halting, she hadn't had enough practice. Or was it that she wasn't as clever as he'd hoped? Had he been mistaken?

Slowly that candle too burnt down, and time, as the phrase goes, "passed, went by, evaporated." Sometimes she missed a line in what she was reading, or she stumbled over a word she didn't know, like "moralize" or "abomination." They plunged her into confusion, and both of them laughed. If someone passed on the dark Gotmarstrasse while they were laughing, Lichtenberg went Pst! and put his finger over her mouth. They sat there, breathing. Outside, the steps faded and finally vanished altogether. If it was raining, they could hear if someone leapt over a puddle. Sometimes he leapt into it, and then he swore. The Stechardess would be standing at his side, "creeping into him." She wanted to show him that, instead of finding it repulsive, she loved his body. "I think it's funny," she said on one occasion. Or else she made a small warm fist and pressed it against his cheek, and Lichtenberg had to ask her forgiveness for laughing about her. Properly, mind, she said, I want you to ask my forgiveness properly!

How?

You have to kiss me, have you forgotten already?

What she preferred to read aloud were fairy tales, or stories that "went on and on and on and never stopped." At the beginning of every new chapter, she said: Hang on! and bent over him to kiss him on the mouth.

In between times, Lichtenberg kept getting sick, sick with happiness, as he said. Then he had to take off his trousers and coat, and lie down. The Stechardess fetched a chair, and sat down beside him. And now, she asked, but he didn't know either. He called for the mirror, and pulled his eyelids down. First he did it with one eye and then the other. What if the sun didn't shine for him one day? Or if it shone, and he couldn't see it?

He started work on an article, "Concerning Some Responsibilities Vis-a-Vis Our Eyes." As he wrote, the Stechardess sat next to him, looking at him apprehensively. He hunkered in the "reading nook" and was very tired. She asked: What are you writing? Won't you tell me?

That day, he was alone in their bed of love. He lay shrouded in the smell of her body. He was so wrapped up in it, it was as though she was lying beside him or on top of him. Suddenly he felt hungry. She had to warm up some milk for him, and pour it into his favorite bowl. He broke stale bread into it, one piece after another. In his right hand, he held his spoon. He stirred with it.

What's keeping you, he cried, and she came in with the honey tub, asking: Do you want me then? He nodded, and she took the spoon and dribbled honey into it. This'll give you strength, she said.

Once he had spilled himself inside her again, he told himself: Now I know her body, so girlish and healthy! Let's see what will happen to it next! Her head he knew just as well. He stroked it a lot. When she stuck it unexpectedly into his study, he looked up from his books and cried: There it is again! meaning her head. When they sat talking about something, he knew in advance "what would come from her next." She knew it with him, too. I knew you would say that, she said.

Oh, he said, really?

Never mind, she said, say it anyway!

Then they sat side by side on the sofa, or at the table. He stirred the honey mash. It was something he liked doing almost as much as writing, perhaps even more. The mash was soft and sweet and slipped easily into her mouth. She sat there beside him with her spoon, which was a little smaller than his. Outside, it got dark.

Once again, he asked.

Yes, once again.

Then they both dipped their spoons. He looked out, where the stars were. He told her about the canopy of stars and the horizon, and as he did he held her hand, kissing it from time to time, or pressing it against his cheek. She didn't understand everything he told her, much of it was too "learned." From time to time, she guessed a bit of it. Since she didn't want to keep asking questions, she nodded a lot. When he talked about his head and his heart, he talked as though of machines.

Why machines, she asked, and Lichtenberg said: Because they're assembled in the same way, and because their constituent parts are not significant either! And he lifted his arm up and down and said: Look at the machine working, see!

The Stechardess laughed to hear the dear man call himself a machine. Sometimes she said: Choo choo choo! and Lichtenberg said: No, don't laugh!

She squeezed his skinny writer's fingers and asked: Are they a part of your machine as well? and he replied: Yes, they're a part of it too! Since she took on board everything he said to her, she started to call him "my little machine," and stroked him over his heart.

My heart isn't where you think it is at all, said Lichtenberg! and she said: Oh yes it is, there! And she lay down with him again, and they played "Beddy-byes."

They were now completely intimate with one another, inside and out. If one began a sentence, the other could finish it. Each knew where the other had what, and what it looked like and felt like. They had long since lost their inhibitions about undressing in front of one another, and running around "in the altogether." Instead of creeping into a corner to strip off her shirt, she said: Look what's coming up next! And with that she took off her skirt and panties, and ran around in front of him all naked and hairless. He sat in his corner, breathing hard and saying: Oh my God, oh my God! Then she skipped up to him and plonked herself in his lap. Or, in a fit of passion, he suddenly stripped the shirt off his hump and shouted: Look, there it is!

But you can hardly see it, she said.

Do you think it's really getting smaller?

It must be! What else could it do?

In their last autumn, Lichtenberg dug into his bag, and with the money he had saved towards a gas balloon, bought himself a new silk coat. This one was in yellow and green. A check kerchief bloomed at his throat, so you could recognize him from a long way away. And that's how he ran around Göttingen. When he passed his neighbors, they nudged each other in the ribs. Look, they said, did you see what just wafted past! One called him "the pocket dandy," another "our little peacock." Lichtenberg in his wig walked silently out of town. Sometimes he had the Stechardess on his mind, sometimes it was the gas balloon. The fine season would soon be over. Red apples and yellow pears glimmered on the trees. If they were hanging far enough down, he would break one off and put it in his pocket. To those he couldn't reach, he said: You're too sour for me! The sweet one he took home with him.

I've got something for you, he cried from the doorstep, concealing it behind his hump. Then the Stechardess had to stand in front of him, shut her eyes and guess what it was. There, he said, and he held the apple up to her mouth. When she had eaten it up, he shook his head. She eats out of my hand, the child, he said. Then she had to get a book, sit down with him and read aloud again. Without turning her into a "sensitive foppette," he wanted to develop her understanding.

But how was that done?

He stroked her little head. Are you making progress in there, he asked, and she said: Yes, thank you very much! He was delighted by the simplicity and directness of her speech, which he thought was "only just that of a child." When she put her book down, and he asked: When are we going to go on! she said: Tomorrow!

Then he undressed her—and she him—and they went back to bed.

Sometimes he would write down one of her sayings, as for instance: "In London, he sat on Shakespeare's chair, and cut off a sliver of it for a shilling." Or he said: "Every day, my darling, you are the object of my most insatiable yearning, sometimes even twice in succession!" She laughed and went into the kitchen. There she was frying and frittering away. Lichtenberg came too. He stood himself next to her and sniffed. His nose has been drawn many times, and a lot of ink has been spilled over it. It was not a thing of beauty. As was the case with all strong characters, there was too much of it, it would have done for two. The bridge was torn, as though someone had given it a yank. People said he could smell anything with it, as far as the next parish. "The aroma of a pancake," he wrote, "is a more powerful inducement to life than all the philosophers' arguments."

Say again?

The aroma of a pancake . . .

They're done, cried the Stechardess, you can sit down now! Shall I unbutton my shirt, to give you something to look at?

Take it off, he cried, take it off!

They ate off the same plate and slept in the same bed. They breathed the same indoor air, and looked at each other in the morning with the same rapture. Each had his own little spot in the bed. That was where they used up their strength and afterwards got it back. With his arm across her titties, that was how they fell asleep. Even though she couldn't sleep well in that position, she didn't mind. If you would put your hand somewhere else . . ., she said, but he said: No, you'd better get used to it!

22.

*L*ICHTENBERG WAS WEARING his wig again—of course. Once again, he set off round the block and through the town of Göttingen. He cried: All those flowers! He wasn't done for yet, as many people supposed, he was still sitting around. When he had written a book and dispatched it to Dr. Blumenbach or Lavater, he wrote in it: "list of errata on erratum slip." He always wanted to be witty. When he left the house at noon, he told the Stechardess what he wanted to eat at night. Sometimes he got home a little late, and his dinner would already be fast asleep. There would be an apple lying on the table in his study. "In the last few years," he wrote, "I have eaten something between five-thousand-three-hundred-and-seventy and five-thou-sand-three-hundred-and-eighty apples, unless I'm mistaken!" A little glass of wine stood by as well, for him to sniff. As he tramped through Göttingen, he carried his stick. He jabbed it into the ground in front of him and "holed it." They were lovely times, perhaps the loveliest. He thought they would go on like that. Because people generally couldn't get enough of him, they all watched him. Usually he only went back and forth between the Gotmarstrasse and the library.

He does that so we see what a lot of reading he does, said one.

And what a clever chap he is!

He keeps needing books, said a third. I'd have thought he'd read enough by now!

Perhaps it's that he loses one from time to time, said a fourth, bringing the episode to a close.

If Lichtenberg was in town when it started raining, he took shelter in a doorway and looked up at the heavens.

There's something coming our way, he said.

Because he was so small—and it appeared he wasn't getting any bigger either—the heavens were a long way from him. And there I was thinking, he said, but once again his thoughts got away from him. He jammed his books in his coat pockets, "making them all baggy." When the Stechardess said: Look what you've gone and done to your coat! he said: Am I meant to have done that? When the rain had stopped, he lugged his books home. If it didn't stop, he said to the librarian: You'd better send me that book, I need it! Tell the boy to bring it over! He won't regret it!

All right, said the librarian, I'll tell him! and the boy duly brought the book. He was wearing shorts, and he carried it first down the Gotmarstrasse and then up Lichtenberg's front steps. At the top, he knocked and called: Here's your book, Professor! Now you can go on reading!

Lichtenberg put his head out of the window and said: Thank you!

Then the boy stood around for a while, taking in all the books that were lying around at Lichtenberg's place. Some were bound in leather, a few even in velvet. The boy stroked them with his fingertips and said: So soft!

Anything else, asked Lichtenberg, who wanted to be rid of him. Oh yes, he said, and he gave him a coin. This includes next time, he said.

Yes, sir, said the boy, I'll try and remember!

He grinned at the Stechardess, and ran out of the house on the Gotmarstrasse. The Stechardess was grinning too. Lichtenberg laid the book on his middle table. He pushed it around this way and that, until it was lying comfortably. Then he returned to his studies. He was back with electricity, which left him no peace. He had got wind of an electrical fish, the electric eel, and wanted to get one for himself, but where was he going to get it from? Search as he might in Göttingen, there were no electric eels. He didn't have much luck in this period of his life. The good Dr. Leibowitz, who just a week before had been alive, was now dead. Then he heard from Ljungberg in Copenhagen that he wouldn't be able to go with them to Italy, he couldn't get time off. "When I heard that," Lichtenberg wrote to Müller von Itzehoe, "I thought the earth would swallow me up. Once again, no Italy for me and a certain other party! Even though I've never been foolish, I know now what it would be like. So I seated myself next to the party in question, so close that I felt her warmth all over my body. I smelt her warmth too. Then we took each other's hands, she and I, and wept. Now I have had this insight, I understand how it must be to lose one's mind." To distract him from his disappointment, the Stechardess brought him a cup of bouillon, kissed him and said: It's all right, I'm just going! Oh, but she didn't disturb him! She was all he had and all he . . .

As already mentioned, then: it was the time of the electric eels. He thought about them a lot. As he did so, he would browse in some book or other, or hunt up or look up something. That's worth pursuing as well, he thought, and read on in some completely different direction. The Stechardess stood in the doorway, looking in on him. She got a piece of paper, and cut it in strips. When he next browsed in his book, she said: Look out! and pushed one of the strips between the pages. Now he knew where he meant to go on looking. Later on, she asked: Are you looking for something again? and Lichtenberg said: Yes, a book! Then he described it to her. She pointed at one, plucked at his sleeve, and asked: Is that the one? and Lichtenberg would either cry: Not now, I'm busy with something else! or: No, I won't read that, it's too small!

You mean the printing is too small, she asked, and Lichtenberg replied: No, the thinking!

I see, she said.

She went back into her kitchen. She was always thinking about him. To help him get his strength back after all his browsing, she made him a soft- or hard-boiled egg, to "make a man of him again." Once, he'd just eaten one, steps came up the front stairs. It seemed they had a visitor. Lichtenberg said: Not another one! and pulled on his wig. Who was it this time?

Do you want me to vanish, asked the Stechardess.

But Lichtenberg said: No, stay!

But then they'll see us together!

Let them!

The sky outside was . . . Well, it just *was*! And the air? That too! Lichtenberg and the Stechardess were dressed in such and such a way, they were wearing this and that. They stepped back from the door so that it could open wide. Would it be a colleague from Hanover, or even from Leipzig? Maybe he had forgotten to announce his visit? Well, let him come! They would take him in their midst, and drag him to their kitchen. There he could wash his travel-stained fingers and sit at the dinner table. They would certainly run to a plate of soup for him. Then Lichtenberg could go to his drawer, take out the little box with the pipes and let the unexpected visitor—could it be Dr. Garve—choose one for himself and . . .

It was no travelled gentleman, neither from Leipzig nor from anywhere else. It was Dr. Gatterer and Dr. Schlichtegroll from next door, both driven by curiosity, and how! They were saying to each other: Now we'll get a good look at her!

At whom?

That woman, of course! Now or never!

They had spent a long time dolling themselves up, inasmuch as that's something a man can do. They had washed themselves with soap, and powdered their brow and cheeks. Such a long time they'd waited! And they didn't want to wait a moment longer. They wanted to inspect the lover of their little friend—"friend"—and not from a distance either, but from right up close!

Everybody knows I ride around on you incessantly anyway, Lichtenberg said to the Stechardess. So why put you to the trouble of hiding?

Whatever you say, she said. Then I won't hide!

Outside, the day was coming to an end. Not again, thought Lichtenberg, as he listened to the two of them climbing up the steps. They walked side by side, they walked, like all good friends, with a single step. Then, as with a single fist, there was a knock on the door. Lichtenberg pulled it open, and the two scholars walked in. They smelled of onion—good for the brain—and of old books. At last we'll get to see his lover from up close, they thought. They had emerged from their respective studies, and were wearing dark frock coats, the most formal ones they had. Under their arms, they carried the books they had just been lecturing on in the university. They were badly used, and would surely soon disintegrate. But that didn't matter, because, as professors, they knew everything by heart anyway. They pressed in through the door.

Good day!

God' ild you!

Salve!

While they were shaking hands with Lichtenberg, they looked around the room. There were the bookshelves, the

grandfather clock, the framed silhouettes, and there . . .
Truly, there was the girl! The Stechardess, who had only very
rarely been allowed to stay in the room when there was a visitor, smiled at the two gentlemen. Yes, so that was her! Dr.
Gatterer and Dr. Schlichtegroll put on serious and dignified
expressions, but they had to admit: Yes, she's quite a looker!
There followed the looking-her-in-the-eye and the squeezing
her hand. Lichtenberg conducted them to their chairs, and
the Stechardess . . . Well, she relieved them of their hats
and cloaks and books, and took them next door. At the
thought that the little Lichtenberg was "in full and repeated
possession of her body," they took deep breaths and started
to sweat. My God, what were they missing! What had they
done wrong in their lives, that they didn't have equally pretty
little things to wait on them in their homes, at least one
apiece? Could it be that . . .

Lichtenberg got his pen and wrote: "If a man has webbed fingers, he is unlikely to make a great flautist!" Then he looked
at his colleagues' flies and wrote: "The smallest junior offi-
cers are the happiest."

And now, he asked.

The Stechardess went into the kitchen to fetch plates and
glasses and the raisin cake that she would occasionally bake
for the little man. See, she said, what I've made for you!

Did you really, he asked, and she said: Did you think it fell out
of the sky, from the middle of a cloud, say? She often used that
sort of tone with him now! At any rate, she put the cake on the
table, and started to cut it up. That brought her into proximity with them again. The two scholars lowered their gaze.

Let's have a bite, then, said Lichtenberg. She's baked it for us, hasn't she?

Yes, said the Stechardess, I baked it for you!

They all brought out their hands from under the table, and slowly began to eat and drink, "because one ought to prolong a pleasure as much as possible." The visitors looked around Lichtenberg's scholarly apartments. Of course they were familiar with them, having been there many times before. But now they looked completely different. A female had established herself there.

The study seemed entirely new. The two chairs, that had once stood far apart, now leaned together. On the low pouffe—his—there were thick cushions, and the windows, which Bain-Marie had only rarely cleaned, now sparkled in the light from the street.

The two visitors sat on their chairs, and were comprehensively distracted. They dropped cake crumbs. Sometimes they dropped a bit, said: Excuse me! and put their feet over it. Instead of keeping an eye on the cake on their plates, they squinnied at Lichtenberg's beloved. And sighed. Sometimes one of them said a sentence, sometimes the other. It didn't develop into any sort of conversation until . . .

We see so little of you these days, said Dr. Gatterer.

True, said Lichtenberg.

But I'm not to blame, said Dr. Schlichtegroll. I often go by your house. And how often I've readied myself for a long conversation, and stood easy, just waiting for someone to knock on my door, and stick his nose in my room, only for no one to knock, no one at all!

Should you have been thinking of my nose, said Lichtenberg: No time, simply no time! I've been, how shall I put it, . . .

Powerfully distracted?

That's not strong enough! You see in me, said Lichtenberg, a driven man! I was . . .

On the way to fame and fortune?

. . . I bumped into something.

What, again, exclaimed Dr. Gatterer.

Did you write a poem, asked Dr. Schlichtegroll.

The time, said Lichtenberg, has not yet come for me to reveal all, but I can promise you: It will come! There ensued another one of the celebrated pauses. They ate and drank and dropped crumbs and sighed and whiled away the time. The hourglass, said Lichtenberg, reminds me not only of the fleeting seconds, but also of the dust into which I shall one day decline!

Me too, said Dr. Schlichtegroll, and Gatterer added: Me too! Then Schlichtegroll asked: So you spend all your time sitting around here and . . .

Yes, said Lichtenberg, and thinking!

And you occupy these rooms all by yourself?

Yes, said Lichtenberg, just she and I! Didn't you know that?

Did we know that, Dr. Gatterer asked Dr. Schlichtegroll.

We didn't, replied Dr. Schlichtegroll, quite know it, but we sort of assumed it!

Is there a lot of talk about us in the town, asked Lichtenberg.

Sometimes!

And what do they say?

I don't know, said Dr. Gatterer, they keep their voices down.

There followed the next lull in the conversation, until Dr. Gatterer exclaimed: Isn't it time for a cork to be pulled with a muffled report?

No, a loud one, said Lichtenberg, getting up.

Or, asked Dr. Gatterer, should the bottle remain corked up in its corner for all eternity?

Were one to trace great deeds and great thoughts back to their source, said Lichtenberg, one would discover . . .

Well, what, asked Dr. Schlichtegroll.

. . . that they all came out of bottles.

Everyone laughed at the witty convolutedness with which the little fellow sometimes expressed himself, on paper and viva voce. He was always at pains to say more than would fit into his sentences. Then, when he heard all that he had said, he got up—"leapt up"—ran over to his desk, and wrote it down. "It's always this way," he wrote: "Someone gives birth to an idea, someone else has it baptized, a third carries his children, a fourth visits him on his deathbed, and a fifth buries him!"

And then?

Then Lichtenberg pulled his watch out of his pocket and looked at it. Aha, he said, and he sent the Stechardess into the cellar where "his best drops were stored, that he didn't let anyone at." The Stechardess fetched a couple of favorite bottles, and brought them to table and . . . It was the day they were all together for the first time. Lichtenberg had laid his hand on the Stechardess's shoulder. There it is, he thought, and there it will remain! They sat so for a long time. No one could see enough of the girl. Finally, Dr. Kästner turned up as well. I thought I'd find you here, he said. He bowed to the Stechardess, and kissed one of her fingers. He wasn't really that bothered about women any more. He was sixty. In bed the previous week, he had felt for the first time the pain in his heart that would carry him off a couple of years later.

Well then, said Dr. Kästner. Well then, repeated Lichtenberg.

23.

*O*NCE WHEN HE RETURNED to the Gotmarstrasse from kite-flying, the "happiest celestial activity I know," he found the boy there who always carried his books home for him. He was standing in the kitchen. He had fetched wood for the Stechardess, and was leaning beside her. Maybe he was even leaning against her. At any rate, the Stechardess seemed to like having him around her. But surely not as much around her as that, thought Lichtenberg, as he stepped into the corridor.

The Stechardess jumped. She sometimes gave the boy jobs about the house. But why always when Lichtenberg was away? She let him peel potatoes or scrub beets or fetch milk from the farmer. Lichtenberg had never paid him any attention "because of the insignificance of his head," but now he noticed this and that about him. For instance that the boy always stood very near his girl. Sometimes they were almost touching. Or did they *actually* touch? Lichtenberg had his wig on, and was carrying some books under his arm. He hadn't been running, but he was panting anyway.

What was that boy's name again, he asked, once he had sent him packing.

Friedrich, said the Stechardess, who was blushing.

What's he doing here while I'm away?

He's only helping me out.

Did you ask him for help?

He volunteers!

And why does he stand so close to you while he's helping?

I don't know!

Well, said Lichtenberg, I don't want him to help you so much! Please tell him that from me! And not so near, tell him! I don't want it!

I'll tell him, she said, and they each went into different rooms.

What else?

What else was going on in the world and elsewhere?

At that time, as ever, there was a good deal of dying going on: Voltaire (1778), Rousseau (1778), Bertin (1790). With the last-mentioned of these, people would shortly ask themselves: Who was that again? Beaumarchais wrote a play and popped his clogs. And that was just the French. Lichtenberg, who kept a "list of the immortal men of my time" in his desk drawer, crossed off all the dead ones and started a new list.

Sometimes, in spite of being so busy, he got bored at home, and said: I need something! God knows what I need, he said, maybe I need more exercise!

Even more exercise?

Let's give it a go!

At such dismal moments, he pulled on his bad weather jacket and fetched his kite, hanging on its wings in the attic. A little wind had picked up, and the weather was perfect. Lichtenberg exclaimed: This is just right! and he trotted out the door with his kite. The Stechardess cried: Are you leaving me again?

Yes, he said, but I'll be back.

And what shall I do in the meantime?

Occupy yourself somehow, my delight!

Shall I cook you something, asked the Stechardess, and he cried: Yes, cook something, cook something!

With his wig on his head he ran up the Masch. There, quite an ill wind was blowing, portending this or that.

Lichtenberg looked up at the sky. A few children chased after him, trying to see his hump. If he ran faster, they ran faster too, and if he stopped, they stopped too. Lichtenberg panted and put his hand over his heart. Then he said: Never mind, I'll do it anyway! and he let the kite go up.

At that time, Lichtenberg was making good progress with his experiments. A speech machine that he had built was able to say the words Papa, Mama, life, death, etc. There was a lot of inventing going on. It stimulated him. For example, he felt close to the inventor Johann Carl Ensden (1759–1849), who was just making his way through Europe with his collection of more than twenty aerostatic figures. These were life-sized creatures, tailored from oxgut and brightly painted—gold, gold! They were suspended from a horsehair, and inflated until they lifted off into the air. Lichtenberg followed them from Göttingen to Hanover and beyond. Everything he noticed about them he wrote down.

So, on his return from such travels, Lichtenberg went kite-flying. Soon the kite was high above him. Because the wind has so much moisture in it, said Lichtenberg, it reduces the electricity. And in fact the wind pulled the kite ever higher, almost up into the clouds. Lichtenberg called it "his beloved big bird." He left it with a boy taller than himself, who had to cling on to it. He held the string looped round his wrist. All of a sudden, the kite went plunging down, and it was hurled against a post. Then, of course, the string snapped.

Oh my God, said Lichtenberg, when he saw his lovely kite hobbling off in the direction of Göttingen, where else. First it turned a couple of somersaults, then it plummeted to the ground.

Oh no!

Oh yes!

They didn't have to look for the torn string for very long. It was lying on the Masch. The children cheered and threw themselves upon it. It was the other side of the town ditch, over the trees on the fortifications. Lichtenberg, his wig all askew, chased after the children. Not so fast! he cried. He was worried about the terror his kite would provoke in the town. Forgotten were Erxleben's death and his own wonderful, now slowly fading love. He stared up into the sky, where his kite had been. Later on, he wrote: "The strangest thing was that . . ." He would finish it at home. After a quarter of an hour, he heard that his kite was stranded on the roof of the wealthy Gumprecht. Half of Göttingen had come out to watch it. Look at that, they cried, see what's fallen out of the sky! "The strange thing," wrote Lichtenberg, "was that if the kite had taken one more little turn, it would have ended up at my window, on my very desk." He sent for the chimneysweep. He arrived in his black trousers and black jacket, and set off up the chimney. To the jubilation of the children, he brought the kite down, and laid it in Lichtenberg's arms. Now what was he going to do with it?

Friedrich was a straight-backed attractive boy with beautiful white teeth, and light, almost blond hair. Lichtenberg didn't care for him. Suddenly he found himself seeing quite a bit of him. Had he not been paying attention earlier, or had the boy not been around then?

Sometimes Friedrich was standing at the back of Lichtenberg's house, sometimes he was hanging around the front of it. He had one leg pulled up and was looking up at the Stechardess's window, maybe she was looking down. Lichtenberg stood behind his curtain, looking down. He listened to the boy's footfall. He observed the glances he sent up to his windows. Sometimes Lichtenberg couldn't stand it any longer. Then he flung open the window and shouted: Hey, you, what are are staring up at me like that for? What do you want?

I don't want anything, shouted the boy, and ran off.

Once, when he was about to run away again, Lichtenberg called: Hey you, come back!

Friedrich put his hand to his chest, and asked: What, me?

Yes, you!

Friedrich came nearer. He took off his cap. Yes, sir, he said. He was talking up at him.

What are you doing in front of my house all the time, asked Lichtenberg.

I'm not doing anything, sir, said the boy.

Then why are you standing there the whole time?

I don't know!

And who are you talking to?

No one!

But I've heard you!

I still wasn't talking to anyone!

Well, said Lichtenberg, keep it like that! Then the little fellow made a big fist, hung it out of the window, and said: Now get lost! He brandished his fist a while longer, and wished it could have been much bigger. The boy had gone red, and he ran off. Lichtenberg took a deep breath and called for the

Stechardess. He was friendly, "but adamant as a morning erection." He took her hand and kissed it and said: There's something I have to say to you, child! Then he explained to her that, because he loved her, she wasn't allowed to look at any other man or "lad," nor stand around with him, sit or stand too close to him, nor touch him, nor allow him to touch her. Do you often stand close to him, he asked.

Not often!

And do you touch him when you do?

No.

What about him? Does he touch you?

Not either.

Inwardly too, said Lichtenberg, you mustn't let him touch you, those inward contacts are the worst. Do you understand me?

I think so!

Good, he said, and went over to the wall. He rubbed his hump. The thought that she might go off with somebody else, even if he was just half-grown, and "allow herself to be touched, or even kissed" by him, plunged him into naked horror. He had been carrying that "perverse notion" around with him for quite a while now, and suffered dreadfully from it. Now he had said it out loud. And yet it was an ordinary day, quite indistinguishable from any other. The most extraordinary insights come to a man on the most ordinary days, he thought, and he began to sweat. He pulled out his handkerchief, and mopped his brow. Even though they hadn't exactly quarreled, it was a bad evening. He had torn his wig off, and prowled around the Stechardess. Did he see something coming? And if so, what? The Stechard was forced to stand in front of him, and swear an oath. She had to swear "never to leave him standing, or in the lurch, never to pass over him or trample about on his heart," and that "she was and would remain his, for all time, and would never, whatever transpired, leave him."

But I'm not leaving you, she said, but Lichtenberg flapped his hand at her and said: That's what they all say! I admit, he said, not necessarily now, but at some stage!

No, not then either!

Oh, he said, that's what they all say!

He went up to the window, and flung it open. He had, as often happened of late, "talked himself into a choleric state." He put his hand out of the window, it was mizzling outside. He draped his wig on, and left the girl. In his sudden fit of jealousy, he walked out of the house. He was heading for a particular place. That's where I'm gimping off to, he thought, through the wind and rain. He didn't have far to gimp. He went to Paris Parva. Usually, he skirted round it, but today he made straight for it.

No, it was not a nice place! And yet it was so close!

"Three steps from my apartments," he wrote to Hufeland, "no, I exaggerate, maybe five, is the end of the world! The dwellings there are like pigsties, truly! They are not more than four or five paces in breadth, the biggest of them maybe six, and all of them are so low that a man of average height— no, not me!—can put out his hand and touch the roof. If you enter such a dwelling, you find yourself in a pig's kitchen. There is one other room, which serves as parlor and bedroom. There the family sit and grunt. You, my dear Hufeland, may imagine, these are no capitalists. By the bye," he wrote, "I am presently engaged upon the difficulties of calculating odds at dice. Back to mathematics then, she awaits," wrote Lichtenberg. He looked around Paris Parva. A bad area that he had walked into, the septic effluents ran into the groundwater. Everything low-lying was inundated. Not at Lichtenberg's, thank God, he lived in a rich part of town! Then, when things had dried out again, the stink of it reached his windows. Normally, when he found himself here by accident, he turned around right away. This time, though, he stuck a clove up his nose, he wanted to see the misery, not smell it! He doled out a few penny pieces, he couldn't stand it otherwise. He thought of his girl, and the petnames he had often given her, things like *heart beetle, tinder miss, little skewer*.

What's that?

My little skewer, he thought.

Then there were the names he had for himself, like *poor neurotic*. "We, by God's disfavor, day laborers, serfs, negroes, villeins and authors . . ." or, if he couldn't think of anything else:

> "The earth quaked
> And was shaked . . ."

What's that?

The earth quaked, thought Lichtenberg, and stamped up the stairs.

Will you swear that you've always been true to me, he shouted into the room and loomed hugely—hugely?—in front of her.

I have always been true to you!

And that you will immediately die a horrible death if you're lying to me!

No, I don't want to swear!

And that you will die a horrible death if you're lying to me!

Oh, she cried, it's all one. I'll swear! I will! I will!

24.

*D*EATH IS AN IMMUTABLE constant . . . Death is a constant . . . Death is . . . Death! What Lichtenberg went through—"suffered," he said—at that time, he couldn't tell anyone. No one was to know how attached he was to her!

Ever since she'd fallen ill, he hadn't left the house. He sat down by the window. Sometimes someone passed on the street below, sometimes he looked up.

Lichtenberg flung open the window and cried: She's in here!

Who is?

My little girl!

Can I see her?

Yes, come on up!

Lichtenberg opened the door and let the man in. He had no words for her condition, or for his own horror and pain. She was now seventeen years and thirty-nine days. His jealousy had vanished as quickly as it had arrived. A "clement mechanism of the brain" would see to it that it remained forgotten.

The Stechard lay all alone in the big bed and no longer looked like herself at all. In just one or two days, she had lost so much weight . . . And that wasn't all! The illness was also in the Dieterichs' apartment on the next floor. There lay Dieterich's daughter Liese, who was three years older, with the same puffy face and the same red splotches. She too was feverish, unable to sleep or wake. Dr. Gatterer put it differently and said: She can neither live nor die!

Help her, please, cried the wealthy Dieterich, pointing to his daughter. The doors in the two apartments kept opening and shutting, because everyone wanted to see the two girls, first one, then the other. Then they talked about them both. At Lichtenberg's, on the lower floor, they put their heads through the door to gawp at the stricken Stechardess.

To get a good view of suffering and decay, said Dr. Schlichtegroll. Then he twisted himself into a corner, pulled out his bottle, and took a gulp from it. Lichtenberg stood beside him, a changed man.

I hope, he said, she won't do anything stupid, I hope she won't die on me! He wanted to add: Because of my stupid suspicion of her! but he didn't say it. Then the doors opened again, and in came some more people wanting to see her— see her die.

Towards lunchtime, Lichtenberg could no longer take it, and his wailing could be heard the length of the Gotmarstrasse.

There is a sick woman here, he cried, get out!

He didn't even wait for them to reply, he pushed them all out. As he went into the passage, he could hear the same wailing at Dieterich's, only from someone else's mouth. Then Lichtenberg had driven everyone out of the apartment, the last of them he bodily thrust out. He was alone with the Stechardess. He crammed his fist in his mouth, and ran around the bed. Once he looked at her a long time, but he didn't come to any conclusions. He pulled back the curtain, so that she could get a good view of him. Then he called her name. Look at me, he cried, can you still see me? For a long time she didn't look. Then he took her by the shoulder and gave her a shaking, and asked if she didn't recognize him.

It was yet again August! It was too hot for her. The women went around in just skirts and blouses, without anything underneath. They stood by the washtubs in front of the houses, and washed a lot. Sometimes they went under Lichtenberg's windows and looked up at him. The men carried newspapers, and fanned themselves. Some said: Well, well! or: This is too awful! or: Who could have seen this coming! Then they looked up at the sky, did they think it would rain at all?

Sometimes the Stechardess opened her eyes, or sometimes just one eye. She looked about her, and with shaky voice, unfamiliarly, called his name. She called him, *dear Master*, as she had at the beginning. Once, the sun fell on her face. Lichtenberg cried: I won't have that! and he drew the curtain. Then she peered momentarily through her grisly mask. By nightfall she no longer knew him. She fingered her blankets and voided into the bed. She began to smell, and talked a lot of rot. Death couldn't be long in coming. Lichtenberg could no longer keep out the people who wanted to watch her die. His room, like that of the Dieterichs upstairs, was no longer empty, just as the world isn't empty but rather the opposite, as Dr. Kästner said, who had also turned up. The room had filled, as though he was to give a lecture. There were her father and her mother, getting in everyone's way, a couple of doctors, whom Lichtenberg had sent for, and whom he would have to pay, two old and five young Dieterichs, who were coming and going and wondering who was doing worse, plenty of neighbors and colleagues who had arrived in the course of the evening and stuck around. They stood among Lichtenberg's equipment, the leaf electroscope and the toothed wheel, filling up his scientific rooms. They fiddled with his apparatus, and whispered to each other. The words that could be made out were all sad. The doctors ran around the Stechardess, applying mustard plasters and Spanish flies. Three times they bled her. They were afraid gangrene might set in, and they wanted to prevent that. Outside, it was getting dark, yet again!

Towards midnight, they turned the Stechardess over, and tore off her nightdress. Then they applied cupping-glasses to her. She no longer knew her mother, not to mention the cripple. He had gone outside. More and more people stood around to watch her die. Then Lichtenberg could no longer take it, he couldn't see her that way.

There are enough of you standing around here waiting, he said to the people, what do you need me for. Now only the doctors are still hopeful, and that's what they're paid to be!

Then he went into a corner, and wrote something in his diary. As he did, he looked right across the room at her. It looked as though he wanted to describe her little face—it had gotten a little smaller still—to the world, once and for all. Or maybe he was writing down something else that had occurred to him. "Are we responsible for the thoughts we have? Are they not stronger than we are," he wrote. Once, he pushed his way through the crowd, crying: She's dying on me, she's dying on me! How can she do it to me, dying on me again? Eternity, he cried . . .

The way she took to eternity was neither the broad, paved one, nor yet the narrow, quiet one, but one in between, where one attracts little attention and is rapidly forgotten.

Lichtenberg had thrown away the colored rags he had loved so much, and went around in black. He watched her funeral from a distance.

When her little hearse took a run-up and trundled through the churchyard gates, he almost yelled aloud.

He could hardly bear to watch them lift her off the wagon. Now his little girl would be melted down, to be restored to the world-machine in some other shape and color and place. When she rolled past him in her coffin, he straightened his wig and slunk away. She was now alone with her mother, a couple of siblings, and an old uncle in "colored clothing." It was all he had. Others were in the St. Johannis cemetery: Dr. Schlichtegroll, Dr. Gatterer, Dr. Kästner, and many, many besides. That was where they were burying the little Dieterich girl. Afterwards, everyone went home from their various burials, small and large, and Lichtenberg became ill. He was now all alone in his part of the house on the Gotmarstrasse, and he said: Nor was that all!

What else is still to come, people asked.

It's already here, said Lichtenberg.

It was a paralysis of the right leg, down to the foot. Lichtenberg cried: Oh my God! and he crept into his bed. Where he had lain Lord knew how often with the little one. He pulled the covers up to his chin, and then up past his chin. Through the window he saw the sun rise more often than set. He had no feeling in the hand that had so often stroked the head of the Stechardess. Everything "was moldering away." In her kitchen too, everything was moldering away. The pots and pans and carving knives that she had so lovingly polished, were now dull and spotted with rust. Dust settled on everything. Sometimes a student fetched up who hadn't heard about Lichtenberg's loss. He walked round the house. Finally he stood at the door and knocked, but no one answered. Then he climbed back down the steps and called up to the window, whether "science wasn't going to be permitted to continue." Lichtenberg stuck his head out of the window, and called: No, not continue! I've put the brakes on it! Then he sent him off home. Then there came high-browed, healthy men, casting covetous glances at his job, and "would willingly teach my children what I teach them, or again perhaps the opposite, in my lecture room, and for my stipend." Instead of directing his focus outside himself, he directed it inside, so that people began to call him the "Columbus of hypochondria."

He started a list of illnesses, all of which he now had: cramps in his belly, *marasmus senilis*—he was all of forty-two!—incipient dropsy, convulsive asthma, creeping fever, jaundice. Moreover, he feared apoplexy and a paralysis of his right side. He thought his veins were knotted, that he had a heart polyp, a growth on his liver, water on the brain and diabetes. In the middle of the night he woke in panic and cried for his Stechardess. He had no picture of her, no drawing, and noticed her vanishing. Strange, after such a short time! Sometimes he went up to the Dieterichs, sat with them and held their hands. They were just as cold as his. After sitting like that for a time, he went back downstairs. When in the course of a conversation—Lichtenberg had sat there in silence—Dieterich said: "I wish God would put an end to my life!" Lichtenberg was so irate that he banned Dieterich from his apartments for some days. Everyone thought his brooding was unnatural. Only rarely, in his better moments, did he have any healthy thoughts. Then he wrote in his wastebook, that he "had eaten Swiss cheese for the first time in months, no, years!"

Since Bain-Marie no longer came, he had another girl to come and do for him.

Can you clean, he asked, and she nodded and said: I can!

What about cooking? Can you cook?

Yes, I can cook too!

Pork belly and beans? Can you cook that?

Yes, pork belly and beans!

All right, said Lichtenberg, let's give it a shot!

Now it was she, instead of the other, dead girl who was standing by his sickbed or in the kitchen. She had a spoon in her hand, and was stirring. Then she took a child's plate and fed him. Sometimes a bit of it trickled out of his mouth. He pointed at it and said: I've made a mess there!

She had tended the sick and the dying. That doesn't matter, she said. Then she got a cloth, and wiped it all away.

Winter was over now. They had opened the windows. They heard the birds shouting. The new girl crouched next to him, and looked at him hard. When he returned her gaze, she lowered her eyes. She was the daughter of a cooper, and her name was Margarethe Kellner (1759–1848). She was much younger than him, though not as much as the other had been. In due course, she would bear him seven, no, eight children. But that's family history, it goes beyond his own personal story, and he said to himself and already he had written it down . . .

And then?

Afterword

*S*OMEONE SAID—YOU CAN probably think of examples—that some or all or most novelists have one novel they keep writing over and over. My father had two. There were the books of generalized or particularized childhood (*Veilchenfeld, Our Conquest*), and there were the books about the problems of art and being an artist (*Our Forgetfulness, The Parable of the Blind,* the long stories about Walser, Lenz, Balzac, Casanova in *Balzac's Horse*). He wrote other books too (*The Spectacle at the Tower, Before the Rainy Season*), but they weren't *his*—or perhaps *him*—to anything like the same degree. Intriguingly, his three last books, *The Film Explainer, Luck,* and *Lichtenberg and the Little Flower Girl* each, in different ways, managed to harness both tropes, art and childhood, and that may be a further reason why I was so determined to translate them. To me, they are a sort of very loose trilogy, and his apotheosis.

* * *

My father was always a writer—long before I was born—but circumstances, job, family, moving around—he was an itinerant professor of German lit., with four children—all conspired against his writing. Perhaps he couldn't see what to do, or what form to do it in. He deliberated. And he wrote plays and a great number of radio plays through the 1960s and 1970s. The result was that when his first prose book was published in 1979—he took his decisive impulse, as a number of

English and American writers have since, from the Austrian, Thomas Bernhard—he gave every appearance of being a late starter. Thereafter, he was always a man in a hurry. He didn't know how long he had left, but he knew it was unlikely to be the 30, 40, 50 years of a standard literary career. He pushed himself. He wrote very nearly a book a year. That's what presumably gave him a stroke at the age of 57—which, typically, he "worked off"—though it left him unable to read—and what killed him, though not until he had written another three books, which for me are the books at issue. *"dieser freundliche, gehetzte Mensch,"* as Michael Krüger his last publisher described him, "this friendly, driven man." The best way out may indeed, with Frost, be through, but through is still, as often as not, out.

*   *   *

Lichtenberg and the Little Flower Girl wasn't intended to be his last book, but—unless he had been spared to write others (he was only 62 when he died)—it is hard to see how it might be improved upon in that capacity. Its last words I don't think can be improved. *Und dann?* And then? It's the sound of his author's engine, Scheherezade almost, still ticking and willing. The manuscript lay completed on his desk when he died on 1 July 1993. The date is Lichtenberg's birthday. (He was 251.) All writers' lives are more or less misshapen and more or less failed; nothing is worth what most of us put into it. Even the poets of war and liberation—Rupert Brooke, Byron, Apollinaire—end unfortunately or tawdrily. I feel nothing but pride and awe for my father, who put himself through these three last books, and ended *Und dann?*

*   *   *

A note on technique. My father's prose is based on the scenes
of dialogue he learned to write in his radio decades. There is
very little description—staple of "classic" novel writing, but
also, in anything less than the most gifted hands, source of so
much ineffable boredom and fatuity for the reader—in his
books. The set-ups are harsh, often confrontational, reso-
nant with pain, humiliation, irony. The speech is jumpy, inci-
sive beyond realism, stressed and tinged with the surreal or
the macabre. If I can have people talking, he once said to me,
I'm away. Over this he applied layerings of what one might
call grammatical varnish. A scene is recollected, written
down, told, played over another scene, (often—I kid you
not!—all four) and you get layer after layer of reported
speech. (Very effective in German, less so in English where
all verb endings sound like the imperfect.) That was also how
they were written, built up and spun out and pasted together
from version to version in the course of very many rewrit-
ings. That was in the early books.

Once he found himself unable to read, my father evolved
a different method, and a whole new style. Where my
mother—indispensable to his whole enterprise, and never
sufficiently to be praised—had previously typed up fair
copies of his manuscripts, she now read drafts back to him,
for him to correct and embellish aloud. Where previously
the star of the show had been the grammar—my father had a
rather undesired reputation for brilliant intricate syntax—
the late books are different. The sentences and paragraphs
are shorter, the confrontations more present, the scenes
seem to ghost in and out, a bigger role falls to diction, to
heckles and interjections, to personality. If the early books

were like palimpsests, stories etched over stories, and all the verb endings and agreements correct and nailed down, the last three seem to float. Switches of speaker and scene, anonymous interjections, an effect of collage, facts and factoids, a strange vagueness or indeterminacy—are we in a one-off or a habitual scene? repetition or variation? it's often very hard to tell—tiny Brechtian or Shakespearian additions of props—the shoe buckles and bonnets here, the wigs and underthings, the meat, the soup, the apples—questions, prompts, exclamations. "It was summer again—or it was still summer." I don't know of anything like them in literature. (Maybe Georg Büchner's extraordinary fragment, "Lenz"; or Penelope Fitzgerald's last, great novel *The Blue Flower,* about Novalis.) I have to say I have loved translating these books, their abruptness, their wild comedy and ringing bathos, their emotionalism and vocal quality. I was working on the first of them, *The Film Explainer,* when my father died. My determination to complete the "set" was as strong as anything I've felt in writing.

*   *   *

A word, too, on Lichtenberg. As you may have gathered by now, not a hoax or an invention. Not a "character," though of course he is that too. Unless you're a Germanist, a lover of aphorisms, or a student of *ur*-science, you might be forgiven for not knowing. A real person. Georg Christoph Lichtenberg. (1742–1799), as my father might have said. The youngest of seventeen children, most of whom died in infancy. Malformed spine. Studied mathematics and science, visited England twice, in the epistolary swim of the international science of the time. A card of the Enlightenment. Further a note-taker and heterogeneous scribbler, who kept what he called *Sudelbücher* or "wastebooks"—the term is from contemporary bookkeeping, a preliminary record of commercial transactions—for his own amusement, never for publication. Goethe, Heine, Schopenhauer, Tolstoy, and Einstein—among others—all championed him later; to Nietzsche his *Aphorisms* was one of the four great books by a German. (They are available in English, warmly recommended, edited and translated by R.J. Hollingdale, in the NYRB classics series.)

Substantial parts of his life and thoughts, as given in *Lichtenberg and the Little Flower Girl,* are "true." Mathematics, science, Göttingen, England, the wastebooks. Some—but not all—of the aphorisms are *echt* and therefore lifted. "A book is a mirror. If a monkey looks into it..." is. "The only manly attribute I have decency unfortunately prevents me from displaying," a little surprisingly, is. "Apparently they're coming back, the birds! It said so in the paper! Not the same ones, of course, Nature's swapped them round," presumably isn't. (The great thing about these isn't their genuineness or not, but their availability as a further form of expression, as a currency—like toy money.) The experiments. The balloons and the electricity. The Lichtenberg figures. The hunchback. The flower girl. Maria Stechard, called *die kleine Stechardin* by my father, in accordance with a beautiful, archaic practice that, along with the definite article, allows a feminine ending,-*in,* to be appended to the surname. Here, the little Stechardess. Their extraordinary cohabitation. ("His private life," writes Hollingdale, quite uncensoriously, in fact, rather tantalizingly, "was very irregular, though not very much more so than that of several even more celebrated Germans of his age.")

ill this, though, is energized and made to work. There can be no greater contrast than that between *Lichtenberg and the Little Flower Girl* and the turgid, research-heavy, imagination-free, historical novel (probably weighing in at a tad under 600 pages) favored in current Anglo-American practice. My father's Lichtenberg keeps bumping against the limits of life: knowledge, law, mortality, infirmity, geography, another person, society, superstition, work. It is even, if you like, a criticism of life, the sort of thing novels used to do two or three hundred years ago. Admirers of the book have said it's the sort of thing Lichtenberg himself might have liked to have written. (As he never went to Italy, or back to England, so he never wrote a novel either.) Reading it back, I see it has something in it of Fellini, whom my father—along with his Kafka and his Mann and his Gogol and his Bacon—idolized. It's probably the zaniest, gloomiest, and funniest thing you've read in a long time, if not ever.

Michael Hofmann
Rutgers University
September 2003